Neighing with Fire

Also by Kathryn O'Sullivan

Foal Play

Murder on the Hoof

Neighing with Fire

Kathryn O'Sullivan

Minotaur Books

A THOMAS DUNNE BOOK
NEW YORK

This is a work of fiction. All of the characters, organizations, and events portrayed in this novel are either products of the author's imagination or are used fictitiously.

A THOMAS DUNNE BOOK FOR MINOTAUR BOOKS.
An imprint of St. Martin's Publishing Group.

NEIGHING WITH FIRE. Copyright © 2015 by Kathryn O'Sullivan. All rights reserved. Printed in the United States of America. For information, address St. Martin's Press, 175 Fifth Avenue, New York, N.Y. 10010.

www.thomasdunnebooks.com
www.minotaurbooks.com

THE LIBRARY OF CONGRESS CATALOGING-IN-PUBLICATION DATA
IS AVAILABLE UPON REQUEST.

ISBN 978-1-250-06641-1 (hardcover)
ISBN 978-1-4668-7419-0 (e-book)

Minotaur books may be purchased for educational, business, or promotional use. For information on bulk purchases, please contact the Macmillan Corporate and Premium Sales Department at 1-800-221-7945, extension 5442, or write to specialmarkets@macmillan.com.

First Edition: May 2015

10 9 8 7 6 5 4 3 2 1

For the Corolla, Carova Beach, and Duck fire departments and first responders everywhere

Acknowledgments

I am always grateful to those who support me as I write, but this was especially true while working on this book. Thanks to my wonderful husband, for nursing me through a month of illness during the writing of this book, serving as my voice, quite literally, when I lost mine, and for reading the early drafts; to my father, for his detailed and insightful feedback that made the book infinitely better; to my mother, for her undying enthusiasm not only for my work but my writing career; to my Aunt Rosie, for inspiring a character in this book just by being herself; and to the rest of my family and friends, for their continued affection and encouragement.

My deepest gratitude to the incredible folks at St. Martin's Press: editor Toni Kirkpatrick, for her vision and kindness; her assistant, Jennifer Letwack, for her dedication and astute notes; publicist Shailyn Tavella, for persistently setting up signings and events; copy editor Edwin Chapman, for his attention to the details; and executive art director David Rotstein, for the lovely jacket that captures the setting so well.

Heartfelt thanks to my agent, Eleanor Wood, for her sage advice and continued belief in me and my work. I'm truly lucky to have her in my corner.

Sincere thanks to all at the Corolla Wild Horse Fund, who are dedicated to protecting the beautiful wild horses and fighting development on the land the horses call home, and to Jim Kelton of Ashville, North Carolina, for adopting Creed, one of the horses featured in this book.

Fond thanks to the independent bookstore owners, especially at Bethany Beach Books, Duck's Cottage, Island Bookstore, Mystery Loves Company, One More Page Books, and Sundial Books, for hosting events, carrying my work, and being delightful people.

A warm hug to the hardworking librarians, passionate book club members, and devoted bloggers, for your love of writers and reading.

Thanks to my writer friends and the fierce women of Sisters in Crime, especially the Chesapeake Chapter, for making me laugh and inspiring me with your stories to be a better writer.

Thanks to reader Shirley Landes, for suggesting Gold-N-Gifts jewelry store. I was delighted to include a scene at the store in the book.

Finally, to the readers who have taken time out of their busy lives to read my books and write me or post your thoughts . . . thank you, thank you for allowing me to share my inner world with you.

Neighing with Fire

Prologue

Sometimes death comes quietly, and sometimes it thunders in on the wave of a tropical storm. Tropical Storm Ana to be exact. After having wreaked havoc as a hurricane in Florida, Ana had been downgraded to a tropical storm and was now hitting the idyllic beach of the Outer Banks village of Corolla with sheets of driving rain and a storm surge that clawed at the dunes.

Sandbags had been stacked at the Monteray Plaza shop doors to stave off the inevitable rush of water. Popular summer hangouts such as Ned's Ice Cream, Corolla Adventure Golf and Bumper Cars, and the movie theater were closed. Vacation homes had been shuttered and poolside lawn chairs and tables tied down. Spray-painted messages on plywood that covered store and house windows ranged from the entreating "Be kind to my cabana, Ana" to the forceful "Go away!" and the downright defiant: "Bring it on!"

A piece of opaque plastic sheeting ripped loose from the roof of a home under construction, made a line drive across the dunes, and then blew high into the air above the crashing waves flooding over beach access points and the two-lane roads that wound through Corolla's oceanfront neighborhoods. The wind propelled the plastic higher, temporarily giving it the same aerial view as that of the Currituck Beach Lighthouse, and then the rain drove the piece down again. The plastic zigzagged up the beach, over where Route 12 transitioned from a paved to a sand road, past the fence that kept Corolla's wild Spanish mustangs within their sanctuary, and into the four-wheel-drive-accessible community of Carova where the horses lived with the piping plover shorebird and sea turtles.

The wind suddenly shifted and the plastic took a sharp turn inland, dipping toward the Outer Banks' second largest living dune, before swirling skyward and heading north. The sheet thrashed over the undeveloped refuge and the occasional house that popped up on the refuge's outskirts and dotted the Carova landscape. Many of the wild horses had found their way along sand roads like Seahorse, Cornflower, and Sandfiddler and sought shelter under the beach homes. Mares and stallions squinted as the wind whipped their manes across their noses; foals huddled against their mothers for protection. Horses not lucky enough to find a safe haven under a house had moved away from the shore and into the maritime woods, deep shrub thickets, or marshlands.

The construction plastic temporarily touched down on the beach, skipped along the shoreline over ancient cedar and oak stumps, buried sea turtle eggs, and the fragile piping plover nests before being snatched from the air by a long nail on a wooden walkway that led from a beach home to the ocean. The sheet flapped violently, fighting to break free, as waves rushed forward to claim the dunes beneath the walkway and drag them into the sea. Little by little, Ana stripped sand from the walkway's foundation, revealing more of the second, original walkway beneath it, and, with every receding wave, unearthed a long buried crime.

Chapter 1

Fire Chief Colleen McCabe pulled her hair from her face, squared her shoulders, and peered down at construction mogul Denny Custis. He sat at a makeshift table made of sawhorses and a sheet of plywood in the middle of the driveway of an oceanfront house under construction. He squinted at a blueprint through a magnifying glass and held up a finger to silence her. She sighed and waited. Her visit with the man had not been going well. She could kick herself for letting Myrtle talk her into it. She was tired from having been up monitoring the storm with the Corolla Fire and Rescue team and the all-nighter was taking its toll. The sounds of hammering, sawing, and drilling weren't helping.

Denny looked up from the blueprint with the magnifying glass still to his face and for a moment gave the impression of a cartoon character with one enormous fish eye. He set the piece down next to a pair of thick eyeglasses, resumed his lunch, and gazed at her.

Denny was not only one of the most powerful men on the Outer Banks, but at six foot three inches tall and two hundred and seventy pounds, one of the largest. He was equal parts gruffness and charm and had a reputation for pushing the zoning limits of what could be categorized as a residence. In Colleen's opinion, his houses were more like hotels. He was also Antonio "Pinky" Salvatore's chief rival in the Corolla and Carova real estate development business.

"If that feeble excuse for a developer thinks he can kill the project," Denny said between bites of macaroni salad, "he's got another think coming." As if for emphasis, he slammed his meaty fist down on a fly that had been buzzing around his paper plate, scraped the dead insect from the side of his palm, and resumed his meal of pulled pork, salad, and sweet tea.

A gust of wind carried a clear sheet of plastic over the dunes. Colleen watched it blow up past the crew working on the third floor of the house and noted the unusually gray June sky above them.

"You sure it's okay for your guys to be up there so soon after the storm?" she asked, raising her voice above the whooshing of the post-storm wind and construction noise.

"You ever heard of a deadline?" he said. "Or would you rather Salvatore be the only one with new homes this summer?"

"This has nothing to do with Mr. Salvatore."

"Yeah?" he said with a raised brow. He gave her a critical once-over. "Ain't that who sent you?"

Her eyes narrowed. "Nobody *sent* me, Mr. Custis. This is part of my job."

"If you say so."

Frankly, she *was* on a spying mission. But it wasn't for Pinky. Myrtle Crepe, Colleen's former third-grade teacher and the obstinate leader of the Lighthouse Wild Horse Preservation Society, had asked her to check on Denny and his activity in Carova after receiving complaints that Denny's crew had been breaking the law by feeding and taunting the wild horses.

The residents of Carova shared the four-wheel-drive-accessible beach with Corolla's horses and other wildlife. While the majority respected their equine, feathered, and furry neighbors, some found them a nuisance. It was the Lighthouse Wild Horse Preservation Society's job to maintain and protect the herd. But every time Myrtle or her fellow officers had driven to the sanctuary to investigate, Denny and his men were well clear of the Spanish mustangs. Myrtle suspected that one of Denny's cronies who lived in the Carova community had been tipping Denny off, and she had repeatedly requested that Colleen pay Denny a visit to see what she could find out.

Since Colleen's and Denny's paths didn't typically cross, and the northernmost beach of Carova had its own fire department, she had had to come up with a legitimate reason to call on him. A recent string of arsons of abandoned properties on the mainland had been the perfect excuse.

"As I said before," she shouted over the miter saws. "I want to"— The sawing suddenly ceased.—"to make sure you have someone looking out for the abandoned houses you're planning to demolish."

Denny snorted. "You amuse me, Miss McCabe."

"It's *Chief* McCabe," she said, annoyed. "And why is that?"

"You actually think someone would try and burn up a place

owned by Denny Custis." He shook his head, wiped his mouth, and snickered.

"There have been three arsons this month. What makes you think your properties won't be targeted?" She winced as hammering began anew on a second floor. "You sure it's okay for your men to be up there?"

"As sure as I am that time is money."

Denny removed a piece of pulled pork from his plate and whistled to Sparky, Colleen's Border collie and constant companion, who was sniffing the nearby dunes. In a flash, Sparky was at the man's side. Denny dangled the meat before the canine. The dog eagerly leapt toward the treat only to have Denny yank it away at the last minute and howl with laughter.

Her eyes narrowed to slits. She tapped Sparky on his rump to get his attention and pointed to her SUV. "Go to the car."

Sparky cocked his head, gazed longingly at Denny's plate of food, and then did as commanded and flopped in the sand next to the vehicle.

Denny popped the meat into his own mouth and grinned at her while chewing.

"You find it amusing to tease animals?" she asked with an edge to her voice.

Denny wiped the back of his neck with a towel, then studied her while taking a long sip of tea. "Why are you really here?"

Before she could answer, a familiar pickup slowed and stopped at the end of the long driveway. Sparky hopped up, barked, and then, recognizing the driver, wagged his tail. Oh no, Colleen thought, and glanced at Denny squinting at the new arrival and reaching for his glasses.

"It appears that person might be lost. I'll see if I can help," she said and tried to appear nonchalant as she hurried away.

As she approached the pickup, her pupils widened. Sitting in the front seat was Myrtle Crepe poorly disguised as a rather eccentric man. Her former teacher sported fake sideburns, the likes of which hadn't been seen since the 1970s, and a dark, thick wig that Colleen suspected came from an Elvis Halloween costume. To complete her ensemble, Myrtle wore a bright orange man's bowling shirt several sizes too large with what appeared to be a pillow stuffed underneath for a belly.

"What are you doing here, Myrtle? And why are you dressed like that?" Colleen asked, irritated that Myrtle's presence might blow her cover. Her brows furrowed. Myrtle's nose was growing longer in the June heat. "What's happening to your nose?"

"Rich taught me last summer how to apply derma wax to make moles and stuff. Pretty good, if I do say so myself," Myrtle said.

Rich Bailey had been the mortician at Bailey and Sons Funeral Services and the community theater's makeup artist until his untimely death last summer. She was certain Rich wouldn't have been impressed with his pupil's skills.

"You're a master of disguise. Are you sure you did it right?" She watched Myrtle's fake nose slowly melting over her upper lip.

"I had to use gelatin, but it works just as well."

"Maybe," Colleen said, pressing on the end of the Silly Putty-like nose to keep it from falling off of Myrtle's face.

"Stop that," Myrtle said, swatting at her hand. Myrtle checked her nose in the rearview mirror. "Now look what you've done."

Colleen glanced at Denny as Myrtle worked on fixing her misshapen snout. Denny squinted at them through his glasses. She positioned herself near the window to block as much of Denny's view of Myrtle as possible. "I thought we agreed you'd stay away," she whispered.

"That's before I remembered how good I am at masquerading. Remember when I was your Uncle Mitch and—"

"Stop!" She didn't need to reexperience the time when Myrtle had shown up at the station in disguise and pretending to be Colleen's uncle. Living through it once had been bad enough. "Listen. You need to get out of here. Denny's shrewd. He'll see through your getup in a second. He already thinks I'm here spying for Pinky."

"Pinky Salvatore? What's he got to do with anything?"

"I was about to find out when you showed up. Now go. You've been here too long as it is. I'll call you if I find anything out."

"I tell you, if he's been hurting the horses—"

"Myrtle!" Colleen said and slammed her hand against the pickup.

"Okay okay. I'm going. But mark my words: if someone doesn't do something about that man, I will." And with that Myrtle hit the gas.

Myrtle disappeared behind a dune. Given how long she had spent with Myrtle, it would be hard to convince Denny that her conversation with the "man" in the pickup had been about directions. Colleen made her way back, unsure of what story would fool him. She had never been good at lying.

"Boyfriend trouble?" he asked with a smirk when she reached him.

"What? No." Clearly Denny was in need of an updated prescription on his glasses. "He was searching for . . . the access road. You know how lost people can get up here."

Denny removed his spectacles and raised a brow. "You and I both know that fella wasn't in need of directions."

Great, she thought. Way to blow my cover, Myrtle.

"I've seen that pickup a lot lately," he added.

"You have?" she asked, concerned.

"Don't you worry. I'm not afraid of some stalker. Probably one of Salvatore's guys. Speaking of which . . . I'm still waiting to hear the real reason for your visit." He folded his arms over his massive chest and waited.

Maybe she was tired of the charade or maybe she was plain tired, but she figured she might as well ask him directly if he had been interfering with the wild horses. "It's about the—"

Sparky woofed. She turned to see Raymond, the famous lone mule in Carova, with three mares. Years ago Raymond had appeared with the herd and attracted his own harem of admirers. He was known to get into scuffles with the larger stallions over territory. Despite the construction noise and Sparky barking and nipping at his heels, Raymond plodded up the driveway toward the property. One of the workers on the second floor of the house whistled and, in violation of the ordinance against feeding the horses, threw an apple down. The mule startled and Sparky growled at the apple as it rolled to a stop. One member of the crew, likely the perpetrator of the apple-tossing crime, laughed at the animals' reactions but the rest shook their heads and resumed working.

"Sparky heel!" Colleen called.

The dog lowered the front half of his body in true Border collie herding mode and stood his ground.

"Sparky," she said again, this time in a stern warning tone, and the dog came running with his tail wagging. She rubbed her canine buddy's side and watched with concern as Raymond retrieved the apple and then withdrew with his harem.

"Stupid fella," Denny said as the mule departed. "Although you gotta admire his way with the ladies."

Her cheeks flushed red with anger. "You know it's against the law to interfere with the horses."

"I'll do what I want—to anything or anyone who comes on my property." He locked eyes with her.

Colleen's heart rate quickened. Was he threatening her?

He heaved his body from the metal folding chair that had sunk into the sand under his weight and pushed his thumbs into the belt loops of his pants. She couldn't help notice Denny's large belt buckle of the smiling Porky Pig Looney Tunes cartoon surrounded by the words THAT'S ALL FOLKS! shining in the sunlight.

"You like what you see?" he said, proudly thrusting his midsection in her direction.

She shuddered slightly in disgust. One thing was abundantly clear . . . Denny lacked any of the chivalry of his rival.

His smile faded to a scowl. "You tell Salvatore I'm not giving up on that property, and he better surrender his claim to it if he knows what's good for him."

What was Denny talking about? She wasn't aware of any property dispute between the two developers. She studied his face.

Perspiration beaded on his upper lip and the left side of his mouth twitched slightly.

"Will there be anything else?" he asked through clenched teeth. "Some of us have work."

She took a slow, deep breath. She had done as Myrtle had asked. She had checked on Denny's construction site and the horses. There was no point getting into an altercation.

"No," she said. "But I suggest you keep an eye on your properties."

"Don't you go worrying your pretty little head about me," he said and held up a fist. "I know this land and the people who live here like the back of my own hand. If something was amiss, I'd catch wind of it."

"Then I won't need to speak with you further." She touched Sparky's neck and turned away.

"Tell Salvatore that if he wants to spy on me he shouldn't send a girl to do his dirty work," he called after her.

She contemplated laying into the man, but instead marched to her SUV, opened the door, hopped in after Sparky, and slammed the door closed. It wouldn't do for her to be Denny's enemy . . . although he had just become hers.

She backed onto the sandy road. It would be good to get away from Denny and the noise of the construction site. The visit had given her a headache. A horn blew signaling the crew that it was time for their lunch break. The hammering, sawing, and drilling ceased. It was then that they all heard it—a woman's high-pitched scream.

She slammed on the brakes. Two workers on the second floor

hurried to the edge of what would soon be a balcony and pointed to a house a short distance beyond several dunes. She hit the gas, sending sand flying, and sped toward the spot.

Two high dunes marked the driveway entrance and made it difficult to see anything but the roof of the house. She parked on the shoulder in case emergency vehicles needed access to the driveway and sprinted toward the sounds of yelling coming from the ocean side. Sparky took the lead and disappeared behind the house.

She rounded a corner and was surprised to find the back area deserted. The sea breeze carried with it excited voices from the beach. She dashed to a flight of stairs that led to the ocean and took the sagging wooden steps two at a time, slipping in the sand that now covered them.

"Stop!" came a voice from below when she reached the top.

She slid to a halt and grabbed the railing to keep from falling. Sparky barked from below and circled a man and woman in their forties and their golden retriever. With one hand the man held the woman's torso in a protective gesture and with the other the golden retriever's collar. The woman stared with her hands to her mouth at the space under the steps.

"Sparky, stay," Colleen said. The dog whimpered but stopped circling and sat next to the golden retriever. "What's going on?" she called to the man and woman.

"It's a body!" the woman blurted out, then covered her mouth again.

"Or what's left of it," said the man.

Had a dolphin or some other sea creature washed ashore in last night's storm? She inched to the end of the walkway, peered over the railing, and tilted her head. Wooden boards from the original walkway were scattered over the sand but she couldn't see anything that resembled a body. Colleen clutched the railing, leaned over it to get a better look, and then saw what had grabbed the couple's attention. Protruding from the area beneath the double walkways was no dolphin or shark but the outstretched fingers of a shriveled and ashen human hand.

Chapter 2

As Colleen helped Bill Dorman, the Currituck County Sheriff with whom she shared a nascent romantic relationship, she couldn't help think that if not for the unusually long-reaching waves of Tropical Storm Ana, the body might have remained safely entombed under the walkway forever. She and Bill tied tarps to metal stakes hammered into the wet beach sand as Bill's deputy, Rodney Warren, finished roping off the perimeter of the wooden stairs. With any luck, their work would protect the body and scene from the weather and prying eyes of vacationers until the medical examiner's team arrived. She gazed at the shoulder, arm, and hand poking out from the sand. Though she was no forensics expert, she guessed that the body had been buried for some time.

"Wonder how long it's been under there," Rodney said softly so as not to be heard by Martin and Laurie Templeton, the couple who had discovered the body.

"The ME should be able to tell us once he's done some testing," Bill replied, also keeping his voice low.

"How long until he gets here?" she asked, and peered at the sun that had broken through the dissipating storm clouds. She wondered what the June heat and humidity would do to the body now that it had been uncovered.

"Let's hope soon, before this draws too much unwanted attention," Bill said, eyeing the observant couple and their curious golden retriever.

"Howdy, folks," came a voice from around a nearby dune.

"Speaking of unwelcome attention," Colleen muttered under her breath, protectively leashing Sparky.

Bill and Rodney looked at her with raised brows. Denny Custis lumbered toward them with one of his goons in tow.

"I'll handle this," Bill said and moved away.

Rodney stepped closer to her as Bill shook hands with Denny. "I take it you don't like Mr. Custis much."

"Is it that obvious?" She had never been good at hiding her emotions.

"Between you and me, I don't have much use for Custis myself."

She was about to ask him why but Bill and Denny were coming their way. Denny's man remained behind and surveyed the beach.

"Good to see you, Rodney," Denny said. Rodney forced a nod. Denny turned to Colleen and added, "Miss."

She folded her arms and squeezed Sparky's lead tight in her hands. Once she had a bad opinion of someone, it took a lot to change it. The fact that Rodney apparently shared her feelings only served to strengthen them.

"I heard the commotion earlier when chatting with the lady here. Came to check out what all the fuss was about."

"You didn't tell me you were talking to Denny," Bill said to her.

"With an arsonist floating around the county, I wanted to make sure he's keeping an eye on his abandoned properties. Isn't that right, Mr. Custis?"

"Whatever you say, darling," Denny said, all oozy, sweaty charm. He peered through a gap between two tarps. "Woowee, seems someone took a dirt nap. That's one nasty carcass."

She studied Denny. Could he really see the body without his glasses? If so, how had his vision improved so quickly from their earlier meeting?

"Any idea what happened?" Denny asked.

"No," Bill said and rubbed his forearm.

The gesture was a sign Bill was uncomfortable with the conversation. Good, she thought. Maybe Bill will get the man to leave.

"How long do you think the fella's been there?"

"How do you know it's a man?" she asked, studying Denny intently.

"I just figured. Not often you find ladies ending up dead like that."

"Not often you find gentlemen either," she said.

"Good point," Rodney said, and stepped a little behind Colleen as if backing her up for a fight.

"Look," Bill said to Denny. "It's too early to know anything. I'm sure you can appreciate the need for discretion."

Denny regarded first Colleen then Rodney then Bill before smiling broadly and patting Bill on the back. "Sure sure, big guy. You let me know if there's anything I can do for you, you hear?"

"Will do," Bill said, obviously not appreciating Denny touching him.

An awkward silence filled the air, and then Denny signaled his sidekick and the two retreated behind the dunes.

Sparky whined to be free of his leash and Colleen released her grip. The dog instantly sprang forward to be with his retriever friend.

Martin Templeton, the man who had discovered the body, put his arm around his wife Laurie. "Gotta say . . . it sure is a strange place to end up dead."

It was true. The body had been buried between a new walkway and the old one that had been covered by the dunes above it. Corolla's and Carova's construction practice of building a new walkway over a preexisting one was a result of the state's Division of Coastal Management regulations that forbid the removal or relocation of sand or vegetation from the primary or frontal dunes. Owners and renters were forbidden from shoveling or sweeping blown or washed-in sand away from or off of the stairs. The stacked walkways up and down the beach made for a peculiar sight. Colleen wondered what vacationers like the Templetons who were unaware of the building codes must think of them.

It was uncertain how long the body had been buried beneath the stairs. But one thing was clear . . . the body didn't get there on its own. Colleen was hardly an expert on the decomposition process but she could tell from the color and texture of the skin that it must have been at least several months. They had had a mild winter, so it was possible that the body had been there as far back as the fall, but she doubted that it had been longer than that given the intense tourist activity last summer.

"We'll need to get a statement from you both," Bill said to the Templetons.

"Sure," Martin said, and whistled for his retriever, who had run off with Sparky up the beach. At the sound of the whistle, both dogs came running.

"I hope you catch whoever did it," Martin said, watching the dogs race to the group, tongues wagging.

"Did what?" Laurie asked.

"Killed him."

Laurie gasped. "You mean murder?"

"What else?" her husband said.

"We're packing this instant," she said and pivoted on her heels.

"I'm afraid you can't leave until we get your statement," Bill said.

"Listen to the sheriff, honey," Martin said, trying to take his wife by the arm.

The woman yanked her hand away. "If you think I'm staying one minute in a house where there's been a murder—"

"We don't know that there's been a murder," Bill interrupted.

"And if there has been," Colleen said, "we don't know that it occurred here."

"Chief McCabe's right. Why don't you two go inside and Deputy Warren will take your statements. I'll join you once the ME's team arrives."

Rodney motioned to the couple. "Shall we?"

Laurie reluctantly nodded and Rodney escorted the couple down the beach to the walkway of the next house and over the dunes. Sparky poked his nose around the side of the tarp.

"No," Colleen said. She took his leash and inspected the body. "Denny's right."

"About what?" Bill asked.

"Our body is a man's. The arm and shoulder are too large to be a woman's." She contemplated the body a moment and then noted Bill's rather calm demeanor. "Does seeing bodies ever bother you?"

He shrugged. "The first few did. It's not that you get used to it but, well, it's part of the job. I'd hate to be a medical examiner though."

"Speaking of the ME," she said, spying the forensic team's four-wheel-drive vehicle carefully maneuvering around parked cars, children building sandcastles, and beach umbrellas. The beach doubled as the official road of the northernmost communities, which necessitated that everyone—whether on foot or wheels—look out for one another.

Bill waved and the medical examiner's crew was soon upon them. The sun's intensity increased as the group methodically marked off the area in preparation for extracting the body. Forensics is a strange science, Colleen thought, as she watched them work and helped Bill keep the area secure.

Garrett Kronzer, the medical examiner, quietly spoke with his team, squinted at the body, and wrote notes in a little book. He was a fair-skinned, bespectacled, slightly built man with close cropped hair who—to Colleen—came across more like a college professor than a medical examiner. He was also rather soft-spoken and serious, which is why she had only had a few conversations with him. On one occasion he had lit up when she had asked him how he determined time of death. He had gone on for a full half hour explaining the experiments labs across the country conducted to study what happened to a body when buried in a variety of soil conditions. Once he had finished his explanation, however, he had become silent and that had been the end of their conversation.

Since he had come on board last summer, the ME had developed a reputation for quick, accurate results. Rumors had it that it hadn't been an easy transition for the new boss. He had led a campaign to overhaul the North Carolina medical examiner system and, in the process, had ruffled a few feathers. Colleen could relate to his struggles. She had had a few of her own when she had first become chief. It was never easy being the new person in charge. But people had to admire his results. She hoped it wouldn't take Kronzer long to determine the manner and time of death for their John Doe.

The vacationing populace emerged from their rental houses to investigate the damage done by Ana and discover what treasures she had left behind on the beach. Before long, Colleen and Bill were busy keeping curious beachcombers at bay. As Bill explained for the umpteenth time what had been unearthed, her thoughts drifted to the body's burial location. She had to admit, it was a brilliant place to hide a body. Anyone who knew about the construction regulations knew that the frontal dunes—and hence the body—couldn't be disturbed. Unfortunately, that didn't help her with a list of possible suspects. Virtually all of Corolla's and Carova's residents knew about the codes. But her mind couldn't help focusing on one resident in particular—Denny Custis.

She found it odd that Denny had come by the scene with his bodyguard, especially since he had seemed so busy and eager to be rid of her earlier. And the sudden improvement in his eyesight was suspicious. Could he really see the body from that distance or did he somehow already know who it was because he was involved in the death? He would certainly know the walkway construction protocols, the location was not far from where she had visited him this morning, and he had additional oceanfront houses under construction nearby. It wouldn't have taken him or one of his henchmen long to dump a body here. If the deed had been done at night or during the off-season, it wasn't likely there would be witnesses. She didn't have proof, but her gut told her Denny was somehow connected to the demise of their John Doe.

Colleen's phone buzzed to life. It was Jimmy Bartlett, her veteran captain and right-hand man at the station. "Hey, Jimmy. What's up?"

"I'm calling to make sure you're still on for the conference call," he said.

"Wow, is it that late?"

"I know you're tied up there. You want me to sit in?"

"Yes, but I'll be there. The ME's about done and Bill's got things under control."

"See you in a few then."

She slipped the phone back into her pocket and made her way to Bill. "I have to get back."

"I figured," he said. "I'm going to see how Rodney's doing with the statements. You want to grab a bite later?" he asked.

Her stomach growled. "Does that answer your question?"

He chuckled. "I'll give you a call then."

She gave Bill a short salute, slapped her thigh for Sparky to follow, and strolled over the dunes on the neighbor's boardwalk to her vehicle. She rolled down the window so Sparky could enjoy the ocean air, drove through the neighborhood to a beach access point, and then headed south toward Corolla.

The wind whipped her hair as she drove down the beach, which doubled as Carova's official highway. She slowed and occasionally stopped for people, dogs, and horses making their way to the water. The speed limit was fifteen miles per hour and she wished that everyone obeyed it. More than once she had seen a horse or child almost hit by someone forgetting that they had to share the beach road.

She was also careful to avoid the ancient cedar and oak stumps protruding from the sand. The stumps were what remained of a maritime forest that had existed some two thousand years ago. They were usually less visible in the summer months when the gentle waves replenished the sand, but some of the larger ones jutted from the earth even during the summer and had been outfitted with red reflectors to warn travelers. Because the storm had washed away much of the sand, there were many more tree remnants than was usual in June and Colleen suspected there would be a lot of vehicle repairs over the next few weeks. When an SUV or pickup encountered the stumps, the stumps always won.

She arrived at the end of Carova where the sanctuary fencing kept the horses safely away from the more-developed neighborhoods of Corolla, rumbled over the steel cattle guard, and drove onto Route 12.

The June sun was shining brightly now. Palm fronds and other vegetative fragments littered yards, pools of water occasionally covered the road, and traffic on Ocean Trail was unusually light for the summer season—all signs that Ana had paid Corolla a visit. Route 12 had flooded during the storm, making any evacuation from Corolla impossible, but it was the dunes that had suffered the most damage. Still, it was nothing compared to what Hurricane Sandy had done back in 2012. Ana had spared the Outer Banks, and for that Colleen was grateful.

She pulled into the Whalehead Station lot. The guys were busy cleaning the engines, picking up storm debris from the property, and hosing sand from the asphalt. Bobby Crepe, the newest member of her team, waved as she parked. Sparky hit her in the face with his wagging tail, eager to be let loose. She opened the door and he took off toward the guys with the hose. They sprayed water into the air and Sparky jumped to bite it. There wasn't a sprinkler or water source that the dog could resist . . . except that of a running bath. Baths he hated.

Jimmy emerged from the engine bay, approached, and squatted next to her back tire. "Looks like you've got a leak."

She removed her sunglasses and inspected the tread. "I think I know why," she said, and pointed to a nail.

"It's in there pretty good. Wonder how you got that."

Her cheeks flushed red and it wasn't from the June sun beating down on the asphalt. "I can't believe him," she muttered and stood with her hands on her hips.

"Who?" he asked, rising and peering inquisitively at her.

"What can you tell me about Denny Custis?"

"Not much, except I hear he's a tough boss to work for."

"Some people say that about me," she said, knowing full well what the guys thought about the tight ship she ran.

Normally Jimmy would have made a wisecrack in response.

Instead he shoved his hands in his pockets and avoided eye contact. There was something more he wasn't telling her.

"Don't give me that look," he said, unable to withstand her scrutiny, and strode toward the station.

She scurried after him. "What aren't you telling me?"

"You're worse than Sparky when he wants a treat, you know that?" he said and entered the shade of the engine bay.

She cut him off and held up her arm to prevent him from maneuvering around her.

"Really?" he said.

"I think Denny may have put that nail in my tire."

He frowned. "Why would he do that?"

"I don't think he took too kindly to a woman questioning the safety of his construction site or questioning him at all. I got a bad feeling about him and I don't think I'm the only one. So if there's something I should know . . ."

Jimmy lowered his voice. "There are rumors that he's used some rather unorthodox methods to get zoning permits through faster."

"What kind of methods?"

"I don't know."

"He did seem concerned about deadlines," she said, remembering her conversation with Denny.

"Not to change the subject," Jimmy said, "but Chip's coming."

"Shoot." She forced a smile and spun to greet her firefighter.

"Hey, Chief," Chip said.

"Hey," she said, stealing a glance at Jimmy, who knew what was coming next.

"You have a second?" Chip asked.

"Jimmy and I have a call about the arsons soon."

"But that's not for a few minutes yet," Jimmy said.

I'll get you, she thought, and sent mental daggers at Jimmy, who grinned back at her like the Cheshire cat.

"What can I do for you?" she asked Chip.

"I was wondering if you had given any thought to Fawn's request. She's been kinda bugging me to ask, seeing as it's next weekend."

Three weeks ago, Chip had announced that he and his girlfriend, Fawn Harkins, were getting married. Fawn was a free spirit and into crystals, tea readings, and tarot cards and last summer had read Colleen's aura and determined that they were bonded in a type of spiritual sisterhood. Fawn had caught Colleen off guard when she had asked Colleen to be one of her "mystical guides into the world of one soulness." At the time, Colleen hadn't even been sure what Chip's pretty girlfriend was talking about and had grumbled that she'd think about it. It wasn't until Jimmy told her that he had agreed to be Chip's best man that she realized that Fawn's "spiritual union ceremony" was, in fact, a wedding and that the young woman wanted Colleen to be the equivalent of a bridesmaid. After last summer's fuchsia cowboy-themed dress debacle, she wasn't sure she was ready for another.

"You're not going to deprive us of seeing you in a bridesmaid dress again, are you?" Jimmy asked, enjoying her discomfort.

Jimmy and Chip chortled. Now you're both going to get it, she thought.

"I appreciate Fawn's invitation, but I'm not really the bridesmaid-dress type."

"That's what I told Fawn," Chip said, undeterred. "But she says you can wear whatever you like; says clothes are just a material shell and don't reflect the true inner beauty of a person. I don't even think she'd care if you wore what you got on now."

Jimmy burst into laughter, then hastily stifled it.

"And what's wrong with what I'm wearing?" she asked, pretending to be offended by the comment about her jeans, station T-shirt, and boots.

Chip's face flushed pink. "Nothing, I only meant . . ."

"Don't you want to dress up for your date?" Jimmy asked, rescuing Chip.

Oh, geez. She hadn't even thought about going to the wedding with Bill as a date. She was still getting used to their shift from being friends to, well, more than friends. The last thing she wanted was for Bill to think she was pressuring him toward the altar.

The phone in her office rang. "That must be the conference call. Shall we?" she said to Jimmy, and made a beeline for her second-floor office.

"But, Chief," Chip called after her. "What do I tell Fawn?"

"You're gonna have to give him an answer sometime," Jimmy said quietly while marching up the corrugated metal steps behind her.

She paused on the stairs. "Fine, fine," she said. "Tell Fawn I'll do it."

"Thanks, Chief! I can't wait to tell her. Oh, you're still helping me pick out the ring Tuesday, right?"

"Yeah," she said, grinning as he bounced from the bay. It was hard to stay irritated at a man so obviously in love.

"Aw, you really do have a heart," Jimmy teased her.

She swiped at him and they ascended the stairs to get an up-

date on the ongoing mainland arson investigations in Currituck
County. Thus far there had been few leads. North Carolina Department of Justice Special Agent Joe Morgan, the lead investigator, was fairly confident that whoever was committing the arsons
was a county resident. The abandoned properties that had been
burned were off the beaten path—an uninhabited house, an overgrown barn, and a long-deserted gas station—and the same accelerant had been used at all three scenes. The fact that the targeted
properties were empty was a relief to everyone as it seemed to in-
dicate that the arsonist had no interest in harming others. In Agent
Morgan's expert opinion, they were seeking a white male in his
twenties or thirties who was only interested in committing crimes
against property. The questions were why . . . and why now?

Colleen was impressed by the investigator's ability to think analyti-
cally about every detail and piece of evidence. From the type of accelerant used to the time of day the crime was committed to the type
of property destroyed, everything told him about the mindset and
behavior of the arsonist. She liked to think that she shared some of
Agent Morgan's analytical skills. But where she differed from him
was in his ability to be nonjudgmental about the act. No matter how
hard she tried, the senselessness and selfishness of a person intention-
ally setting a fire got under her skin. Maybe it's because the thought
that someone would unnecessarily create an environment that might
take a firefighter's life was not only criminal, it was recklessly immoral.

While the motives for arson typically fell into one of six catego-
ries, the cases she was aware of only fell into one of three: profit in
the form of fraudulent insurance claims, revenge or anger against
a neighbor or former lover, and vandalism by teens. From what she

had learned on the conference call, profit was out as a motive as the only connection the properties had was that they were all situated in Currituck County. It was unlikely that they were set as an act of revenge as the properties' owners were all different. A teen or group of teen vandals seemed the most likely culprits. She had even known a few childhood friends who had liked to set fire to leaves with magnifying glasses. Special Agent Morgan, however, wasn't convinced that it was teens. He finished his update somewhat abruptly and the call was over.

"What did you think?" Jimmy asked when he was sure they were disconnected.

"Agent Morgan is sharp. He'll get the guy. Let's just hope it's before the arsonist strikes again."

"You think we have reason to be concerned?"

"There's always reason to be concerned when it comes to arson," she said. "But it appears unlikely he'll come over the sound to the islands. There aren't as many abandoned properties here and we have tens of thousands of people visiting every week."

"Which means tens of thousands of potential witnesses," Jimmy said.

She nodded. "So, how about you help me change that tire."

"Hey, Chief," Chip called up the stairs.

"Not again," she said.

"You got a visitor."

She descended the stairs with Jimmy, spotted Myrtle waiting in the bay sans disguise, and groaned.

"There you are," Myrtle said.

"I'll take care of the tire," Jimmy said with a grin, knowing full well how Myrtle could get under his boss's skin. "Good to see you again, Mrs. Crepe," he said all syrupy sweet as he passed Myrtle on his way outside.

"Hmpf," Myrtle said, aware that she was somehow the subject of a joke.

"What happened to your nose?" Colleen asked, unable to resist ribbing her former teacher.

"It fell off, no thanks to you."

Colleen chuckled, picturing the fake nose plopping into Myrtle's lap.

"Yes, very funny, go ahead and laugh. I'll have you know I worked hard on that nose."

"How long have you been dressing up like that?" Myrtle waved the question away like it was an irritating nat. "And stalking Custis?" she asked, amused at Myrtle's refusal to answer the question.

"Who says I'm stalking him?"

"He does."

"Not everything is about that man," Myrtle said, exasperated. "Sometimes people have other reasons for going undercover."

"Really. Such as?"

"Such as . . ." Myrtle began but then, unable to come up with an explanation said, "Such as none of your beeswax. You always were nosey."

She had been an inquisitive kid and sometimes that curiosity had caused her trouble. She hated that Myrtle could pull out her childhood and use it against her when needed. "Perhaps I've learned to mind my own business," she said, determined not to let Myrtle bug her.

"That'll be the day."

"From what I saw this morning, it looks like the pot is calling the kettle black," she said, teasing Myrtle.

"What I do is investigation."

Colleen sighed. They could go around in circles like this all day. "I'm a little busy, Myrtle."

"Busy with your boyfriend, Sheriff Dorman," Myrtle said. She wrapped her arms around her back and made kissing noises.

"Stop that," Colleen said, yanking Myrtle's arms down. She looked out at the lot to see if any of her men had seen or overheard Myrtle. They hadn't. "Bill is not my—" She caught herself. Why was she even getting into this with Myrtle?

"Mother," Bobby said, coming around the corner. "What are you doing here?" His cheeks flushed pink and he lowered his voice. "I thought I told you not to come by."

"I'm not here to see you," Myrtle said.

Bobby glanced at Colleen, mortified. "You can't bother my boss either."

"Before Colleen was your boss, she was my student."

"It's okay," Colleen said to Bobby. "Why don't you go help Kenny with cleaning up out back."

Bobby nodded, flashed Myrtle an expression of irritation, and exited the engine bay.

She considered telling Myrtle that her visits only served to give the guys material with which to rib Bobby but knew it wouldn't do any good. Myrtle did what Myrtle wanted.

"I'm assuming you're here to find out about my visit with Denny," Colleen said once she was sure Bobby was gone.

"I'm not here to exchange pecan pie recipes," Myrtle snorted. "So, let's have it."

Better to tell Myrtle and get it over with. "When I was at Denny's, Raymond came onto the construction site with his harem, which I thought was strange given all the noise. Then one of Denny's crew threw an apple to him. The way the mule responded, I don't think it was the first time."

"I knew it," Myrtle said, triumphant. "I can't wait to see his face when I give Custis the fine."

"Don't you have enough battles going on right now?"

"What battles?"

She wasn't sure if Myrtle was playing dumb or whether her former teacher had been clashing with so many people that she didn't know to which fight Colleen was referring. "The one between you and the piping plover folks."

"Ridiculous," Myrtle said. "To blame the horses for the nest destruction when those dinosaur-sized Tour-zilla trucks are rolling through the dunes ripping everything up."

Over the last few months, Myrtle had become embroiled in a struggle with those protecting the piping plover. From what Colleen had heard, the piping plover advocates were insisting that the horses were trampling the bird's fragile nests, which the birds built in the sand along the edge of the dunes. Myrtle insisted that it wasn't the horses that were damaging the nests but the vehicles of one particularly aggressive horse tour company owned by the Snelling family. Duck hunters had soon taken sides with the shore bird defenders and now everyone was fighting over who had priority to the land that was shared by all involved. Colleen understood why

Myrtle was against the Tour-zilla company with its oversized trucks, but she couldn't understand why the two groups devoted to protecting endangered species couldn't get along. Things had become a real mess, so much so that it had made the local news.

"You can understand why the piping plover folks have concerns," Colleen said.

"Did Rosalinda get to you?" Myrtle asked, pointing an accusatory finger. "Whatever she said, it isn't true."

"I've never met Rosalinda. All I'm saying is that I understand their concern for the plover."

"Whose side are you on?"

"The side of harmony," she said with a sigh. "Now, if there's nothing further . . ." She held out her arm to usher Myrtle from the garage.

"All right, all right," Myrtle said. "No need to bum-rush me."

Colleen smiled despite her annoyance. She never could predict what would come out of Myrtle's mouth.

"Tell your boyfriend, Sheriff Dorman, I'll be calling him about the citation," Myrtle said loudly over her shoulder as she walked past Colleen's men.

The men peeped at one another and snickered.

Colleen turned away before they could see her cheeks redden. Geez. What was it with everyone teasing her about Bill? Was it so wrong to want to keep some things private? The one person that she knew she didn't have to worry about razzing her was, of course, Bill. She was looking forward to having dinner with him. There was nothing better than sharing a meal with someone with whom you could fully be yourself.

Chapter 3

"*To truly eat well* in the Outer Banks, one should dine at The Blue Point," Colleen had told visiting friends many times and, as Bill pulled into the parking area, her stomach growled with anticipation of a meal at the restaurant.

Bill crept along searching for a parking space in the lot of Duck's Waterfront Shops, a quaint boardwalk shopping village that was home to over a dozen boutiques, eateries, and The Blue Point. He passed what was once the Powder Ridge Gun Club—a waterfowl hunting club built in the 1920s—that was now Duck's Cottage Coffee and Books. Duck's Cottage was a favorite stop for vacationers and known for its delicious coffee, tea, and pastries, its diverse selection of newspapers and books, and the pond behind it where children fed fish and ducks.

"The place is packed," Bill said.

"We can always go to Metropolis if we can't get in," she said,

untroubled. She was just enjoying the fact that they were out together after her busy afternoon.

Once Myrtle had departed, she had spent the remainder of the
day doing a review of Tropical Storm Ana damage, preparing for
the upcoming Junior Firefighter Game Day, and tracking down
when the new engine would be arriving. She had dropped Sparky
off at home, fed him and her Siamese cat, Smokey, and changed in
time for Bill's arrival.

She was still adjusting to Bill picking her up rather than meeting him places. She had been on her own for so long that it was
strange to have someone looking out for her. On more than one occasion, Bill had had to fight to get her to allow him to help her with
something. The most recent example was when she had been re-
pairing loose boards on the pier that led from her house to the Currituck Sound. It had taken three rather forceful offers from him
before she finally conceded that the task would go a lot quicker if
she let him help.

It was good to have him back in town. He had been one of
a select group of law enforcement officers invited to attend a
prestigious training detail on homeland security and terrorism
and had been away from mid-November to the beginning of
March. While Bill was gone, they had talked on the phone reg-
ularly, sharing stories about their lives that, prior to last summer, they had kept to themselves. In some ways, his absence
had brought them closer . . . and, Colleen had to admit, her
heart fonder.

"Here we go," Bill said, finding a spot at the far end of a row.

"Now let's hope we can get in," she said. She hopped out and slammed the door.

There was a reason The Blue Point's parking area was packed. The restaurant featured Southern cooking with local, sustainable seafood, the best seasonal ingredients, a tasty blue margarita, and spectacular sunsets over Currituck Sound. Colleen reached for the restaurant's doorknob but Bill beat her to it and held the door open for her. Yes, she was still getting used to things like that.

"Have anything available for two?" she asked the young woman at the entrance podium.

"It's a thirty minute wait," the hostess said in a Ukrainian accent.

Colleen suspected the woman was one of the many exchange students from Eastern European countries who came to work in the United States each summer. Colleen found the Outer Banks to be the most beautiful place in the world, but she often wondered if the exchange students were disappointed that their opportunity to see America ended up in the Outer Banks of North Carolina rather than New York City or Los Angeles.

"Do you want to wait?" asked the hostess.

Before they could answer, an exuberant "Chief McCabe! Sheriff Dorman!" filled the air. Colleen, Bill, and the other patrons turned to see what the commotion was about and spotted Pinky waving from a booth by the window.

"I think we'll join our friend," Colleen said to the hostess, and then whispered to Bill, "I'll explain why later."

She knew Bill wouldn't be excited about sharing his dinner date with Pinky, but once she had a chance to explain to him the conversation she had had with Denny earlier and Denny's accusation that she had been spying for Pinky, she thought he'd understand.

"So good to see you both," Pinky said as they reached the table. "Care to join me?"

"Dining alone?" Bill asked, noticing the table had only one place setting.

"Not now," Pinky said with a smile, gesturing for them to have a seat.

She took a seat opposite Pinky. Bill slid in beside her.

Seconds later, the waitress approached their table. "They're joining you?" she asked Pinky.

"Yes," Pinky said, and flashed her one of his minty fresh smiles. "If it's not too much trouble for you, of course."

"Not at all," the waitress replied.

She had to give Pinky credit . . . he certainly knew how to charm the ladies.

"So can I get you two anything to drink?" the waitress asked Colleen and Bill.

"An iced tea for me," Colleen said.

"I'm fine with water," said Bill.

"Oh, come now," Pinky said. "Why not join me in a drink?"

"I'm driving," Bill said, still not pleased to be dining with Pinky.

"What about you," Pinky asked her.

She wanted to say yes but thought it better to be clearheaded when she asked Pinky about Denny. "Iced tea is fine."

"One water, one iced tea," the waitress said. "I'll give you time to check out the menu."

Colleen watched the waitress make her way to the bar. She wondered how to broach the topic of Denny with Pinky. She sensed it might be a touchy subject.

"What are you thinking about?" Bill asked her.

"I know that look," Pinky said, teasing. "It usually means the lovely chief is about to interrogate me."

She wrinkled her nose, annoyed but not entirely angry that Pinky had been correct. It gave her the opening she was hoping for. "Tell me about Denny Custis."

"See?" Pinky said with a triumphant grin.

Bill frowned. He was not enjoying Pinky's flirting or the fact that he didn't know what Colleen was up to.

"I understand there's a dispute over land," she said.

"Custis is a vulture," he said with disdain. "He wants a property I own."

She tapped Bill's foot with hers, her way of signaling him that this had been the motivation for dining with Pinky. Bill's shoulders relaxed and he leaned forward with interest.

"Custis seems to think the land is his," she said.

"Because he's a greedy—" Pinky stopped himself. "The records prove the land is in my company's name."

"Then what's at issue?" Bill asked.

"An entire parcel. One, I might add, that would be large enough to build a hotel on if not for a certain piece that I own right in the middle of it."

Pinky pounded the table with a finger then glanced out the window. It was the first time she had seen genuine anger from him. The two rivals obviously shared a mutual dislike—if not outright hate—for one another.

"Where is this land?" she asked, curious as to where Denny wanted to build a hotel this far north.

Pinky paused, and then said, "Carova."

Bill's brows furrowed. "Doesn't sound like a solid plan given that the area is only four-wheel-drive accessible."

"You think that wouldn't change once he got ahold of the property?" Pinky said, locking eyes with Bill to drive home the point.

"But that's where the horses are," Colleen said, horrified by the idea of a hotel in the midst of the horses' last refuge.

"Which is why he'll get that property over my dead body," Pinky said and meant it.

Most people in the community had no knowledge of Pinky's incredible generosity when it came to helping the wild horses. He had never admitted to making the large donation last summer, but Colleen and Bill had figured it out. She admired Pinky for wanting to remain an anonymous benefactor. He could have made a big show of it, won over some of his detractors, and even shown up his stingy rival Denny, but by remaining anonymous, he had kept the focus on the horses.

"How long has your feud with Mr. Custis been going on?" Bill asked.

"A feud goes two ways," Pinky said. "This is not a feud. He's tried vandalizing my properties, hiring people to squat on them, even tried having one condemned but, contrary to what I know some people think of me in this community, I don't stoop to criminal tactics."

"How come I haven't heard about this?" Bill asked. "You could file a complaint."

"I'm not the type of man that lets others settle matters for him."

Pinky's animosity toward Denny strengthened the negative opinion Colleen had formed of the construction kingpin this morning. And no wonder Myrtle was unhappy with Denny. Not only was he possibly interfering with the horses, he was threatening to take away part of their habitat and bring in roads—the very thing the horses had been moved away from when relocated to Carova.

"I'm afraid all this talk about Mr. Custis hasn't made me good company," Pinky said, removing his wallet and leaving a fifty-dollar bill on the table. "Please, take my table. Enjoy the view. It was nice seeing you both again." And with that Pinky made a smooth but hasty exit.

She and Bill sat in silence for a moment.

The waitress returned with their drinks. "Something wrong?" she asked, noticing Pinky's absence.

"Our friend had to go," Colleen said. "But we'll be staying for dinner." She took the fifty-dollar bill and held it out for the waitress. "He left this for you."

The waitress's eyes widened. She scanned the exit for Pinky and then turned back to Colleen and Bill. "So. What can I get you two?"

They placed their orders, more preoccupied now with the conversation with Pinky than with what delicious food they put into their bellies. Bill waited until the waitress had left and then scooted to the opposite side of the booth to face Colleen directly.

"Were you spying on Denny for Pinky this morning?" he asked.

"No. I didn't even know about Denny and Pinky's dispute."

"But you *were* snooping." Her lack of denial gave him his answer. "Who for?"

She exhaled. There was no use hiding it from him. "Myrtle."

"Myrtle?" he said, surprised.

"She believes Denny or his men are harassing the horses, but she hasn't been able to catch them. She thinks he has scouts to alert him when she's touring the refuge."

"He probably does," Bill said. "That still doesn't explain your involvement."

"Myrtle thought Denny's men wouldn't be on the alert for me."

"So you came up with the story about checking on his properties because of the arsons as an excuse."

She knew that tone. It was the one Bill had when he thought she was butting in where she didn't belong or intruding on one of his investigations. "So you know, I was rewarded for my good deed with a nail in my tire."

"You probably picked it up at the construction site. That happens a lot."

"Must be," she said, not wanting to tell Bill her theory that Denny or his goon had done it to punish or warn her. She didn't want him to worry, especially when she didn't have any proof Denny was responsible. Time to shift attention away from her covert operation. "I got the impression this morning when we were with our John Doe that Rodney isn't too fond of Denny."

"Really?" he asked, and took a sip of his water. "Did he say something to you?"

"Only that he didn't care for him. I thought you might know why."

"No. But it sounds like a lot of people don't like Denny."

"How about you?"

"I try to leave my personal feelings out of my dealings with people."

Her eyes narrowed. "So you didn't mind him slapping you on the back and calling you 'big guy'?"

His jaw clenched. "Denny's the kind of man who has to let other men know he's in charge. I don't get into it with people like that."

"Funny. You and Pinky seem to be in agreement about how to handle Denny."

"Could we please not talk about Salvatore?"

"We do have him to thank for this great view," she said, and pointed to the sun setting over the sound. "You gotta admit that."

"Maybe."

The sun painted the sky a brilliant fiery orange before disappearing over the treetop horizon of the mainland. The food arrived and they dug into delicious dishes of freshly sautéed trout, beef tenderloin, and roasted potatoes. After a few minutes of eating in comfortable silence, Colleen leaned back, feeling pleasantly relaxed.

"You didn't say how things went with the couple who found the body," she said as Bill finished his meal.

He took a sip of water but said nothing.

"Oh, come on," she said. "We're not going to do this again, are we?"

"It's our pas de deux," he said.

"Our what?"

"Nothing," he said and blushed.

"No. You said it's our pas de deux."

"If you must know," he said, finding it hard to keep a straight face now. "Pas de deux is a ballet term."

"Really?" She suppressed a giggle. "And how, might I ask, do you know this? Have you been watching _Dancing with the Stars_ or something?"

"I got dragged to my sister's dance recitals for years. There's a set order to the dance steps and it always ends the same."

"Okay then, smarty pants. Since you know our 'dance' always ends up with us working cases together, why don't we skip the middle steps and you tell me what the Templetons said and if you know any more about our John Doe."

"So we're like Nick and Nora Charles now?"

"Or Castle and Beckett."

Bill grinned. He's really enjoying himself, she thought. She folded her arms and feigned impatience.

"There really isn't much to tell," he finally said. "The Templetons went outside to inspect the beach after the storm and when they got to the bottom of the walkway discovered the body."

"They hadn't noticed anything unusual about the dune before the storm?"

He shook his head. "Before the storm they said the entire area under the walkway had been covered by sand."

"You have any outstanding missing persons reports?"

"No," he said, and rubbed his arm.

There was something more. She leaned forward and studied his face intently. "You don't seem too eager to find out who our John Doe is."

"I'm sure we'll hear soon."

"No," Colleen said. "That's not it." Her eyes widened in sudden understanding. "You already know who he is."

"What makes you say that?"

"All the years we've been working together. Who is he?"

Bill squirmed under her gaze. "Michael Hector Fuentes."

She didn't know if she was more stunned by the news that their John Doe had a name or by the fact that Bill had known and hadn't told her.

"Still no word on cause or time of death," he said before she could ask.

"That's got to be a record for the ME," she said. It hadn't even been twenty-four hours since they had recovered the body. "How'd they ID him so fast? The body looked, well, bad."

"The guy had a pacemaker. As soon as the ME saw that, he entered the serial number into the registry and got his name."

"The name Michael Fuentes doesn't sound familiar. You think he was visiting on vacation?"

"Could be. He's not in the missing persons database. I've had Rodney put the word out and make some calls. See if anyone knows him."

If Fuentes wasn't a local then how did he end up in Carova buried under a walkway that someone knew couldn't be disturbed? Was he at the wrong place at the wrong time? Had he been up to something illegal? And why hadn't anyone come forward searching for him? The more they found out about the dead man, the more they'd learn about the possible identity of his killer.

"What are you thinking?" Bill asked.

"If Mr. Fuentes wasn't a local, whoever killed him certainly was, or is."

"We don't know that we're dealing with a homicide . . . not officially anyway."

"Last summer and now this. I'm starting to wonder if Corolla has become a home for murderers."

"No more than any other community," he said. "A forensics lab director once told me anyone is capable of anything . . ."

". . . under the right circumstances," she said, finishing his sentence. She had heard that said as well.

The waitress approached. "Can I interest you in coffee or dessert? The chef's made a key lime pie to die for."

"Not for me, thank you," Colleen said, certain she couldn't squeeze another bit of food into her belly.

"Just the check," Bill said, and the waitress handed him the paper, already anticipating his answer. He slipped her a credit card and she disappeared to ring up the payment.

They settled the bill, then went north on Route 12 to Colleen's house. Bill made the turn off of Ocean Trail onto Lakeview Court and then into her driveway.

"Care to come in for coffee?" she asked.

"Coffee would be great," he said and cut the engine.

She exited and closed the door. Bill's phone buzzed to life.

"What's up," she heard him ask as she crossed to his side. Through the open window, she heard Rodney on the other end say something about speeding. "On my way," Bill said and hung up.

"You've got to go," she said.

"Some kids are racing motor scooters on Ocean Trail between Duck and Pine Island."

She shook her head. That stretch of the two-lane road was winding and had lush foliage from the wildlife preservation center on both sides, which made seeing around the bends difficult. If anything, it was best to slow down in that section.

"I'm sorry you can't come in," she said, trying to hide her disappointment.

"Me, too," he said softly.

Her cheeks flushed pink. These were the moments that were still awkward for them. When they were "just friends" she would have pounded the side of his vehicle and told him she'd see him later. Now all she wanted was for him to stay.

"I gotta go," he said, breaking the silence.

"Be careful," she said, then thought how stupid the comment was since it was unlikely he'd encounter danger from teenagers on scooters.

Bill flashed a smile, leaned through the window to give her a kiss, got pulled back by his seat belt, and grazed her cheek with his lips. They chuckled at the uncomfortable moment. His phone buzzed again.

"That's probably Rodney," she said. "Let me know if you hear anything more about Fuentes."

He nodded, started the engine, and maneuvered out of the driveway. She watched the emergency lights flash as he disappeared around the corner, then listened for his siren to kick on before going inside. One of these days, things aren't going to be so awkward between us, she told herself.

Chapter 4

Sparky and Smokey stared intently at the two bowls of food in Colleen's hands, prompting her to recall the twentieth-century philosopher Martin Buber's saying, "An animal's eyes have the power to speak a great language." She wasn't sure how "great" the language her furry friends were speaking to her right now was, but it was crystal clear.

She set down the food—Fancy Feast Ocean Whitefish and Tuna for Smokey, Beneful Beef Stew for Sparky—and sank onto the kitchen floor, exhausted. She leaned against the refrigerator and observed her companions savoring their meals. Smokey briefly looked up while licking away a bit of food from her mouth, blinked a "thank you" to Colleen, and then returned to her dish. She rubbed the cat's ears. Even though the chatty Siamese could annoy Colleen with her habits of sleeping on the dining table, jumping on the kitchen counter, and occasionally swiping at Colleen's foot, Smokey was a loving kitty. And there was no sound she enjoyed more than listening to Smokey's loud purr while falling asleep.

Sparky slurped up his food and then ogled the cat's dish. Colleen admired her canine companion's intelligence and loyalty. Unlike other dogs, Sparky wasn't prone to making fast friends with every dog he met. In fact, quite a few dogs annoyed him with their enthusiastic sniffing and jumping. It had surprised her when he had taken to the golden retriever on the beach this morning. He could be cautious with people, too, until he trusted them. He had even been guarded with Bill at first—hard to believe now given how much he enjoyed Bill being around since his return to town in March.

Since Bill's homecoming, she and he had been redefining what exactly they were to one another. She didn't know why the transition felt so awkward. She had had boyfriends before, even lived with one. But this was different; Bill was different. He was her best friend. She didn't want to mess that up. She suspected that he might be feeling the same, and it was for these reasons they had moments like the clumsy kiss good-bye.

She had had to adjust to Bill stopping by the station. When he did, she felt like all eyes were on them . . . and many times they were. Jimmy must have sensed this because one day he had taken her aside and told her all the guys were relieved that she and Bill had finally acknowledged what everyone had been able to see for some time. Jimmy was a good guy . . . even if he did tease her unmercifully.

Smokey finished her meal and retreated to the living room for her post-dinner bath. Sparky licked clean the cat's plate, then trotted across the foyer to join his feline friend. She rinsed the dishes in the sink, placed them in the dishwasher, and plodded into the living room to watch television. She surfed the channels and found a news reporter interviewing a local painter and sculptor named Autumn about her work. She propped herself on the sofa pillows, listened to the artist, and drifted off to sleep.

Colleen's cell phone buzzed. She groaned and blinked into the light streaming in through her living room curtains. Her head felt like it weighed fifty pounds. She forced herself upright and discovered Smokey and Sparky staring curiously at her. A local weather person was predicting a sunny, hot day on the television. She clicked the TV off. Had she really spent the entire night on the sofa?

She retrieved the phone from between the cushions. "Hello?"

"Good morning," Bill said on the other end.

She heard the sound of a car pulling up to the house.

"Hey," she said, rising to find out who would be coming by this early.

A door slammed and footsteps crossed the porch. Sparky lowered his head and growled at the knock on the front door. Smokey scurried under a side table. She peeked out the curtains and Bill waved. She hung up, brushed back her hair, and wiped the sleep from her eyes before opening the door.

"Please tell me that's coffee," she said, eyeing a large Styrofoam cup of steaming liquid in his hand.

"And doughnuts from Lighthouse Bagels," he said holding up a white paper bag.

She moved aside to let him in. Sparky wagged his tail and sniffed at the bag.

"Sparky, go find the rabbit," she said, and the dog hurried outside to make his morning rounds and search for the elusive rabbit that lived on her property.

"Are those the clothes you were in yesterday?" Bill asked, more an observation than a question.

She closed the door, took the coffee from his hand, and trudged into the kitchen to get a plate for the doughnuts.

"Everything okay?" he asked, following her.

Smokey emerged from her hiding place, scampered to Bill, rubbed against his legs, and yowled.

"All right, all right," Colleen said, opening the cabinet to retrieve food for the cat.

"Why don't you let me feed Smokey," he said, grabbing the can from her hand. "You work on waking up. I've got news."

"News?" she said. "What news?"

"Drink the coffee and have a bite of that doughnut. Then I'll tell you."

"What is it?" she asked, impatient to hear what had brought him by so early.

"Eat," he said, motioning to the bag.

"I know how to take care of myself." She grabbed one of the restaurant's famous homemade doughnuts and took a big bite for emphasis.

"Yes," he said with a grin. "But I need that mind sharp and awake."

Bill's recent caregiving behavior could be wonderful . . . and downright infuriating—especially when she knew he had big news. She took another bite of the scrumptious doughnut and her irritation with him disappeared. Lighthouse Bagels & Deli really did make the best bagels, doughnuts, and breakfast in Corolla. She watched Bill feed Smokey, then smiled with appreciation when he joined her at the table.

"Good," he said. "You awake?"

She took a swig of coffee to wash down the doughnut. "Let me hear it."

"The ME's office called about Fuentes. Preliminary findings suggest proximate cause of death was strangulation. Apparently the hyoid bone in Fuentes' neck was fractured."

"So it is murder," she said.

"That's not all. Fuentes was one of Denny's workers. Last time anyone remembers seeing him was back in December."

"Why didn't anyone report him missing?"

"Turns out he doesn't have any family in the States. When Rodney talked to some of the workers yesterday, they said they thought Fuentes went home to visit family in Mexico and decided not to come back."

"An immigration issue?"

Bill shook his head. "Fuentes was legalized and a decorated Afghanistan war vet."

She stood and paced. "Don't you think it strange that Denny didn't wonder why one of his guys stopped reporting to work?"

She could see Bill wanted to counter her argument. It was part of what he had called their pas de deux—telling her not to jump to conclusions, asking her if it was her gut rather than her head telling her this—but instead he surprised her.

"I do," he said, rising. "Which is why I'm on my way to talk to Custis now. Fuentes may have told Denny why he wasn't coming back."

She walked Bill to the foyer. "That doesn't make sense. Why wouldn't Denny tell his guys, then?"

"Maybe it was personal and Fuentes didn't want anyone knowing."

She opened the front door and stepped onto the porch. "Something isn't making sense here."

"Again, why I want to talk to him," Bill said, reaching his vehicle.

"I'll ask around the station to see if anyone has heard anything about him." Bill's brows furrowed with concern. "Don't worry. I'll be discreet."

Sparky tore around the corner, tail wagging, and paws and fur wet. He shook and sprayed them with a mist of brackish water.

"He's been in the sound again," she said by way of apology.

"He needs a b-a-t-h," Bill said, knowing if he said the word it would send Sparky running.

She grabbed the dog's collar to keep him from rubbing against Bill. "Call me after you talk to Custis. Thanks for breakfast."

He gave her a quick peck on the cheek. She held onto Sparky as Bill drove away, and then hurried inside to get ready for work. She took a quick shower, left Smokey sunning upstairs under an open bedroom window, and headed to the station with Sparky. With any luck, one of the guys might have heard of Michael Hector Fuentes.

Colleen made her way down Route 12. There were already a lot of cars on the road—residents heading to work and visitors making up for the day they had lost on their vacation because of the storm. She stopped to let bikers cross the road to Currituck Heritage Park and peered up at the Currituck Beach Lighthouse. People were already at the top, taking pictures and enjoying the spectacular view.

A woman with a stroller hurried from the parking lot of the shops across from the park to take advantage of the break in traffic. The plywood over the windows was gone and the spaces in front of OBX Barbecue Stand were full. OBX Barbecue Stand had made its debut in April and had been an instant success. The smells of pulled pork and barbecue chicken floated through the open window causing Sparky's nose to twitch and his mouth to salivate. She inhaled deeply. It did smell good. Maybe they could stop by the stand on the way home and pick up dinner. The neighborhood was bustling with activity. She sensed today was going to be eventful.

She half expected there to be an emergency at the station when she pulled in, but all was quiet . . . eerily so. Like the calm before the storm, except the storm had already passed. Sparky sensed her tension and licked her chin as she threw her SUV into park.

"Bill's right," she said, gently pushing him away from her face. "You need a b-a-t-h."

The dog wagged his tail, blissfully ignorant of the future bath plans, and jumped from the vehicle after her. She slammed the door closed and made her way to the engine bay. The engines and ambulance gleamed. She inspected the garage . . . spotless. Not a piece of equipment was out of order. Still, she couldn't shake the feeling that they should review the equipment again.

Having organized everything late last night and then again at the shift change this morning, she knew the guys would grumble about another equipment check being unnecessary. And they'd probably be right. Maybe it was the fact that the arsonist hadn't struck in two weeks—the longest hiatus between incidents—that was putting her on edge, or maybe it was the news that Michael Fuentes had been murdered, or maybe it was simply that she had had a bad night's sleep on the sofa, but she couldn't shake the feeling of something looming on the horizon. No, it wouldn't hurt to do another check—just in case.

Colleen opened the door and entered the community room. Kenny and Bobby were playing Scrabble at a table, Chip was passed out on the sofa, and Jimmy was in his office doing paperwork.

"Hey," she said, joining Jimmy. "How are things?"

"Pretty quiet," he said.

"A little strange, right?"

Jimmy set down the paper. "What's on your mind?" The two had known one another for quite some time. He could always tell when something was bothering her.

She shrugged.

He raised his brows, folded his arms, and sat back in his chair. "That bad?"

"Just a feeling. Probably the doughnut I ate this morning," she said, trying to lighten the mood.

"Doughnuts, huh?" Jimmy chuckled. "That doesn't sound like you."

She smiled but decided not to tell him that the doughnuts had been a breakfast treat from Bill. "Tell me something," she said. "You ever heard of a guy named Michael Hector Fuentes?"

He shook his head. "Who is he?"

"The guy that was found under the walkway. Nobody seems to know much about him."

"There are a lot of rather reclusive types in Carova. I imagine a person could stay pretty anonymous up there if he wanted to."

"Maybe," she said, remembering she had told Bill she'd be discreet. "Anyway, the reason I came to talk to you is that I'd like to do another equipment—"

He never heard her last words. Their pagers shrieked to life and their cell phones buzzed with an incoming text. Seconds later the dispatcher informed them over the pagers of a house fire on Sandcastle Drive. Bobby and Kenny leapt from the table, Chip bolted from the sofa, and she and Jimmy dashed into the engine bay.

Her men suited up and started the engine. Sparky barked as she hurried to her SUV. "Go to your bed," she commanded and pointed inside. Her heart broke at the sad face he gave her, but he did as instructed and retreated to the firehouse. She didn't want to be distracted by Sparky being near the danger. Her men would need her full attention.

She opened the back of her SUV, tied her hair back at the nape of her neck, and retrieved her chief's helmet. The engine pulled out and the ambulance followed. She soon caught up with the ambulance and engine.

The emergency vehicles slowed in order to make the sharp right off of Route 12 onto Headwind Way and then a quick left onto Sand-

castle. Sandcastle Drive was located in the northernmost community of Corolla, ran parallel to Route 12, and was lined on either
side with beautiful oceanfront and oceanview homes. Kids often
rode bikes on Sandcastle; she hoped they were all off of the road.
Several people on balconies pointed down the road directing the
engine. A band of teen boys raced alongside the engine—something
she, too, had done as a child whenever there was a fire in her apart-
ment complex—and then were soon left behind.

Black and gray smoke billowed across the Columbia blue sky and
out to sea in a menacing plume. It wasn't difficult to trace its ori-
gins to the windows and roof of an oceanside residence near the
end of the road. Colleen parked behind the ambulance as the engine guys threw trucks under the tires, pulled hoses, and retrieved
irons and self-contained breathing apparatus. The blue plastic
coating on the windows and the Dumpster in the driveway confirmed that it was a house under construction. The initials "AS"
on the side of the Dumpster indicated that it was one of Pinky
Salvatore's.

She eyed the smoke engulfing the neighboring house and yelled,
"Jimmy, evacuate the house next door."

Jimmy nodded to Chip, who sprinted to the neighboring house
and helped evacuate the residents to a safe distance across the street.
Moments later, flames shot through a window of Pinky's building,
raced up the side of the house, and stretched toward the house next
door, just out of reach.

"Did you get the man out?" the attractive woman in her thirties asked Chip as he helped her and her son.

"What man?" Chip asked.

"The one that was in that house," the woman said, indicating the burning building.

Colleen's heart skipped a beat. Someone was inside. "Send rescue in," she called, and Jimmy signaled Chip and Kenny, who were already positioning their oxygen masks over their faces. They grabbed their tools, a thermal imaging camera, and rushed to the burning structure.

"Give 'em some help, fellas," Jimmy said to Bobby and the guys on the hoses.

Her men opened up the nozzle and aimed the water toward the flames as their comrades entered the house. Colleen bit the inside of her lip. It was a nervous habit she had whenever her men were in danger and wouldn't go away until they were all out safely.

The wooden dwelling was burning fast, and because much of it was still under construction and open to the elements the flames were getting plenty of oxygen. Colleen scanned the crowd for the woman who had reported seeing a man inside.

"You said you saw someone inside?" she asked the woman. "Are you sure?"

The woman nodded. "He was talking with another man not too long ago."

"He was yelling at the funny-looking man," interjected the woman's child.

"There were two men?" Colleen asked.

The woman gestured for her son to be quiet and said, "The other man left."

"Thank you," she said and joined Jimmy.

"How are they doing in there?" she asked with concern.

"They haven't found anyone," Jimmy said.

The walkie-talkies buzzed with static. "It's getting pretty hot in here, Chief," she and Jimmy heard Chip say.

Chip wasn't known to show concern about his own safety, especially when he thought someone was inside. The fact that he was mentioning the heat told her he was worried. She hated pulling her guys out but it was preferable to going to one of their funerals.

"Time to get out, Chip," she said into the walkie-talkie.

"On our way."

"They're coming out," Jimmy called to the rehab team, the crew responsible for tending to the health issues of the firefighters.

Bobby and the other guys on the hose were winning the battle with the fire on the side of the house. The house next door would be spared. Chip and Kenny emerged from the front of the house, dashed down the steps, removed their oxygen masks, and took bottles of water from the rehab team. Chip was exhausted and, Colleen knew, disappointed that he hadn't come out with anyone alive. She made eye contact with Jimmy, who was talking with Chip and Kenny. Jimmy gave her a thumbs-up that they were okay.

It took her men about an hour to extinguish the fire completely, after which they went inside to check for any rekindle and to open up walls. With the ground saturated from the tropical storm, it hadn't taken long for the water from the hoses to transform the street into a two-inch-deep river. The house would need to be torn down, but she was proud that her men had managed to save enough of it that evidence as to what started the blaze might still be present.

"Hey, Chief," Bobby called from the doorway of the house.

"What is it?" she asked, gazing up at him.

He held his arm at his side, pointed his index finger toward the ground, and waved the hand two times. The hair on her neck stood on end. This was a signal that her firefighters had created for occasions when talking might be difficult or undesirable, and one that none of them ever wanted to use or see. It meant Bobby had found something . . . or rather someone.

"I'm gonna take a look inside," she said to Jimmy.

Jimmy crossed to Rodney Warren, Bill's deputy, who was talking to vacationers standing across the street, tapped Rodney on the shoulder, whispered in his ear, and nodded toward Colleen. Rodney scrambled across the street to join her.

"Mind accompanying me inside?" she said, trying to appear casual and keep her voice low.

"Not at all," Rodney said, and trailed her up the front steps.

"It's toward the back," Bobby said when they reached the threshold. He pointed to the right near where the kitchen would have been.

Colleen crept toward the area. She noticed a trail of charred wood. "Streamers," she said, more to herself than to Rodney.

"What?" he asked.

She indicated the narrow trails. "Someone set this fire. Probably with gasoline or kerosene. Helps it spread from one area to another. Those trails are what arson investigators call streamers."

She tracked the streamers, keeping her eye out for any sign of an accelerant. The smell of wet, burned wood filled her nostrils and permeated her clothing and hair, and the moisture in the air felt heavy on her skin. She reached the back of the house, peered around the corner into the kitchen, and discovered a scorched body.

"Oh geez," Rodney said, and turned away.

Her heart sank. She had been hoping that the woman and boy had been wrong about someone being inside. She inched her way into the room and twisted so as to inspect the body straight on. The body was on its back with its feet facing the door and its arms out at its sides. From the size, Colleen could tell it was a man, but beyond that the fire had made the person impossible to identify. She sighed and removed her cell phone from her pocket. Time to call Special Agent Morgan . . . and the ME. She was about to dial when something familiar caught her eye. She leaned over the body and focused on the midsection.

"What is it?" Rodney asked, keeping his focus up in an attempt to avoid seeing too closely the burned body.

Though it had been discolored by the fire, the object at the middle of the figure was unmistakable . . . a smiling Porky Pig belt buckle.

She looked at Rodney lingering in the kitchen doorway. "I think we found Denny Custis."

Chapter 5

The scorched beach house teemed with investigators—some from the medical examiner's office and some from Special Agent Morgan's arson investigation unit. Colleen remained with Kenny and Bobby from her engine crew to keep watch for any rekindle while the rest of her men had returned with Jimmy to the station for future calls.

Bill and Rodney were busy keeping visitors and the press outside the perimeter. They had blocked off access to Sandcastle Drive from Route 12 to prevent a bottleneck, but the press had parked their satellite trucks on the shoulder of Ocean Trail and trudged across the median to report on the fire and the discovery of a victim inside. She and Bill had only had time to exchange quick hellos.

"Chief McCabe, Agent Morgan would like to speak with you," called a man from the arson investigation unit.

Colleen strode toward the house. Agent Morgan's appearance was every bit like she had imagined from the phone conversations— tall, with graying hair, a moustache, glasses, and a modest navy suit. She had also observed him to be thoughtful, confident, and serious. But that's where the accuracy of her predictions had ended. She had had an initial meeting with the arson investigator when he had first arrived on scene to go over her observations and had discovered him to be a bit quirky. After conversing with her briefly, he had abruptly turned and entered the house with his team to investigate and collect evidence.

She entered the house. The body had been removed and was on its way to the medical examiner's lab to confirm its identity and determine cause of death. But Colleen didn't need verification of the victim's identity. The belt buckle was good enough for her. She had shared with the ME's team what the neighbor had said about an argument with another man, and the medical examiner dictated a note to himself on a recorder to look for signs of a struggle. Everyone involved knew this was a major event. If the arsonist from the mainland had struck again, then he had added homicide to his criminal repertoire.

"Chief McCabe's here," the man said as they reached Agent Morgan. He retreated to continue evidence collection.

Agent Morgan stood completely still with his back to her. She waited, not wishing to interrupt whatever it was he was doing. The silence continued. She glanced at the members of the arson investigation team to see if anyone else found the behavior unusual. Nobody did. They were too preoccupied with putting pieces from the flooring into sealed metal containers, photographing the streamers, and searching the grounds for an igniter or an object that had contained the accelerant.

"Chief McCabe," Morgan finally said without turning around.

"Yes," she said, carefully stepping forward.

"Your thoughts?"

She wondered what more she could tell him about what she had observed. Her hesitation got his attention and he rotated to look at her.

"Not about the evidence," he said. "What are your thoughts about this scene?"

"I'm not sure what you're asking," she said.

He sighed, unaccustomed to having to explain himself. "Your gut, McCabe. I'd like to know what your gut is telling you."

Her brows raised in surprise. She had heard Morgan was a guy who firmly believed that the evidence, not speculation, was what mattered. Maybe she had heard wrong. "My gut tells me that it's arson and that—"

"No no," he interrupted, frustrated. "Do you think this is our guy from the mainland?"

"What? Oh. I don't know. You'd know best."

"Never mind," he said, and walked away into the kitchen where Denny's body had been discovered.

Her cheeks flushed with irritation at the tone he had taken and his sudden exit. She peeked at Morgan's team. If they had been surprised by the conversation she was having with their boss, they didn't let on.

"Excuse me," she said, pursuing Morgan into the kitchen. "You want to know if I think it's your guy. No. I don't. It's all wrong."

"What is?" he asked, any crossness now gone.

"The place, the MO, the fact that there's a victim."

He smiled slightly and nodded. "It's a different shark."

Why was he mentioning sharks?

"Jaws," he said. "You know the movie. They catch a shark, but it's the wrong one."

Agent Morgan may be a brilliant arson investigator, she thought, but he was proving to be one odd fellow. "Yeah," she said. "I guess I think he's a different shark."

"Good. Thank you. That is most helpful."

"Are you saying we have two arsonists?" she asked.

"Or a shark that's changed his eating habits."

She waited for him to say more, and then realized that that was the end of the conversation. "Thank you for driving over and adding this to your caseload," she said.

"It's what I do."

She had never considered herself a poor conversationalist, but around Morgan she felt at a loss as to how to respond. She quietly left the eccentric investigator with his thoughts.

"Let me by," Colleen heard someone say with urgency as she emerged from the house. She recognized the voice, squinted into the sea of emergency vehicles, satellite trucks, and spectators, and saw Pinky pushing against Rodney's outstretched arm.

She scurried down the steps, squeezed through the crowd, and paused upon reaching Bobby.

"It reminds me of when I saw mother's house in flames," Bobby said, observing Pinky with Rodney. Last summer, Myrtle's house had caught on fire after a gas explosion. "I feel for him."

"I know you do," she said. She patted Bobby's arm and proceeded toward Pinky and Rodney.

Colleen eyed the reporter from WAVE television doing her stand-up on the other side of the caution tape. Having overheard Pinky's outburst, the newswoman had stopped her report and crossed toward Pinky. Uh oh, Colleen thought, and maneuvered her way through the emergency vehicles in Pinky's direction.

"Sir," the reporter said to Pinky. "Did I hear correctly? You're the owner of this house?"

"Yes," Pinky said, letting go of Rodney to talk to the reporter.

"Could I have your name?"

"Antonio Salvatore."

Colleen stepped between Pinky and the reporter. "I'm sorry, but I'm afraid I need to speak with Mr. Salvatore." She took Pinky by the arm and pulled him away from the reporter and toward the house.

"Chief McCabe! Do you think the arsonist has struck again?" called the reporter.

"They think this is arson?" Pinky asked Colleen.

"Keep moving," she said. "Can you get Bill?" she asked Rodney as she passed by with Pinky.

"On it," Rodney said and made his way to where Bill was busy protecting the scene.

"Would someone tell me what's going on?" Pinky said as she guided him to the dunes at the side of the house.

She turned to Pinky and looked him in the eye. "I need to ask you a question and I need you to be straight with me."

"I've never been anything but."

She hesitated, not sure how to ask Pinky without upsetting him.

"What is it?" he asked with concern.

"When was the last time you were at this property?"

"Yesterday."

"You haven't been by here at all today?"

"No."

"Are you sure?"

"I think I'd know whether or not I'd been here," he said, slightly indignant. "Wait. You don't think I set this fire, do you?"

There was no way Pinky would destroy something he took so much pride in. "No," she said. "I don't."

"Did some of your men get hurt?" he asked, concerned.

"No."

"Then would you care to explain why you've dragged me into the dunes with that serious expression on your face?"

"You haven't heard anything about what's happened here?" she asked.

"I've been attending to other matters. I didn't know what was going on until I heard a woman at the gas station talking about a house fire on Sandcastle. That's when I drove up."

Pinky's story didn't seem complete, but she believed that he hadn't known about his house being on fire.

He studied her. "There's something more going on here than the fire."

"Why don't we wait until Bill gets here, then you won't have to repeat everything."

"You mean then you won't have to explain our tête-à-tête in the dunes," he said, and raised a brow suggestively.

"This is hardly a tête-à-tête," she said with a grin.

"Then what is it?" Bill asked, coming around the building.

"Bill," she said, her smile disappearing. "We've been waiting for you."

Bill eyeballed Pinky. "Of course you have."

"Chief McCabe has some questions she'd like to ask me but wanted you around for the answers."

"I have a few questions I'd like to ask you myself," Bill said, and folded his arms across his chest.

"Such as?" Pinky asked.

"When was the last time you saw Denny Custis?"

"I thought I made it clear at dinner the other night that I want nothing to do with that person," Pinky said.

Her eyes narrowed. One of the qualities she admired about Pinky was his ability to keep his cool in most circumstances. Even now, with his oceanfront property ruined, he hadn't lost his composure—not really. But the mere mention of Denny irked him. She wondered how far Denny had pushed him to get this reaction and what Pinky might have done if he had finally had enough.

"The people next door said they heard arguing between two men some time before the house caught fire," Colleen said.

"There you have it," Pinky said.

Bill sighed. "Have what?"

"Isn't it obvious?"

"Isn't what obvious?" she asked.

"This," Pinky said, gesturing to his ruined property, "has Denny Custis written all over it."

"That's an odd choice of words," Bill said.

"It's his style," Pinky said.

"It's also your style, if I'm not mistaken."

All three knew that Bill was referring to Pinky's old habit of burning debris as a way of luring Colleen to pay a visit to his trailer.

"Look, Sheriff," Pinky said. "If you want to know who set this fire, then put out an all-points bulletin for Custis. I guarantee he's behind this in some way. Now, if there's nothing further, I have to call my insurance company."

"Not so fast," Bill said, blocking Pinky with his arm. "How much insurance did you have on this place?"

"Is he serious?" Pinky asked Colleen.

She nodded.

"It's a common motive for arson," Bill said. "Were you or were you not at the house arguing with Denny Custis this morning?"

"I don't understand why you keep coming back to that."

Colleen noted Pinky's perplexed expression. Could it be? Had Pinky not heard about Denny's demise in the fire? "He doesn't know," she said to Bill.

"I don't know what?"

"Don't go anywhere," Bill said, and abruptly walked away.

"What's going on?" Pinky asked.

Bill made his way into the crowd. Moments later he emerged with the woman and boy who had witnessed the man arguing with Denny before the fire. Bill pointed at Pinky and Colleen. The boy and his mother looked in their direction.

"Why do I feel like I'm in a lineup," Pinky said.

Because you are, she thought, and held her breath. Seconds later the boy and mother shook their heads, and she let out a silent sigh of relief. Pinky was not the man that had been fighting with Denny. Bill patted the boy on his back, shook the woman's hand, and rejoined Colleen and Pinky.

"They couldn't make an ID," Bill said to her.

"He's going to find out," she said. "Isn't it better he hears it now than on the evening news?"

"You know, I'm right here," Pinky said, waving his hand between them. "Would you two stop being so cryptic and tell me what's going on?"

Bill paused and then said, "Someone perished in the fire. Colleen thinks it was Custis."

Pinky's normally tan face paled.

"Are you okay?" she asked. Pinky took a deep breath, nodded, and color returned to his cheeks. "Any idea what he might have been doing in your house?"

"He's vandalized my properties before, mostly stealing copper piping and tools, but I never thought he'd . . ."

The sound of the ocean filled the silence.

Pinky cleared his throat and collected himself. "I'd like to go if that's okay with you."

Bill studied Pinky a moment and then said, "Do us a favor. Don't mention any of this to that reporter. We still haven't had an ID from the medical examiner's office."

"Of course not," Pinky said. He forced a smile at Colleen and then disappeared around the side of the house.

Pinky was many things, but he wasn't a murderer. Right now, however, he was the only person with a strong motive.

"You think Pinky's right? That Denny's responsible for the fire?" she asked.

"I don't know. But I do wonder what he was doing on Salvatore's property."

She poked at the sand with her foot, lost in thought, and kicked a piece of litter into the air. She noted the garbage and was annoyed to see that it was three attached matches. Now who would smoke and throw that on the ground with dune grass nearby? Didn't they realize it could start a fire? Her eyes widened. She squatted and examined the spent matches. "I think Agent Morgan will want to see this."

Bill surveyed the ground, spotted the matches, and disappeared around the front of the house. Minutes later, he returned with the investigator.

"I understand you've found something," Morgan said.

She pointed to the ground. Agent Morgan examined the matches, took a photo, and then carefully placed them into a metal container.

"They were under the sand. You think it's the igniter?"

"If it is," the agent said, "it's a different shark." He flashed Colleen the briefest of closed-lip smiles and marched away.

"What's he talking about sharks for?" Bill asked.

She spotted Rodney jogging toward them. "I'll fill you in later."

"Hey, Bill," Rodney called from the corner of the house. "The press wants a statement."

Colleen groaned.

"Tell them we're coming," Bill said. The deputy nodded and jogged away. "We should get Agent Morgan."

"Something tells me he's not the press conference type," she said.

"Do you want to do it?" Bill asked.

"How long have you known me?"

"I'll get started then," Bill said, knowing of her distrust of the press, and strode toward the crowd while she went to retrieve Morgan.

The press conference was brief. Colleen confirmed that they had found a victim in the fire, Bill handled questions about the possibility of the death being a homicide, and Agent Morgan refused to speculate if the mainland arsonist had struck again. She had been relieved that he didn't bring up the shark theory. Afterwards, she consulted with Morgan, left two guys at the site with the engine on the first shift of the twenty-four-hour rekindle watch, said goodbye to Bill, and headed back to the station. She was anxious to find out how her men were doing—particularly Chip and Kenny, who had been inside the burning structure. Responding to a call that involved a death was never easy.

Chapter 6

"You're not Superman," Fawn said to Chip with tears in her eyes. "You don't have a cape."

"I got something better," Chip said, stealing a look at his fellow firefighters, who were checking equipment in the engine bay and pretending not to hear his conversation with his fiancée. "I got turn-out gear."

Colleen and Jimmy exchanged a knowing look. This was one of the hardest aspects of the job—helping significant others understand why firefighting was not only an occupation, but a calling.

"Aren't you proud of me?" Chip asked.

Fawn caressed his cheek. "Of course I am, Chipmunk. I just don't want to lose you."

"I got a great team here," Chip said, gesturing to the room.

Colleen and Jimmy pretended to study paperwork as Fawn

scanned the group. They peeked back in time to see Chip take Fawn's chin in his hands and lift her face to his.

"Can't I put out any fire?" he asked.

The room fell silent. Everyone felt the pain of the situation and the importance of the moment. Fawn stared into Chip's eyes.

"Except the one you started in my heart," she said, and kissed him deeply.

Someone called "Get a room!" and Fawn and Chip smiled sheepishly. Colleen heard Jimmy sniffle and caught him wiping his eyes.

"Are you crying?" she teased.

Jimmy wiped away a tear. "Better watch out. I'll start calling you Cold-Hearted McCabe," he said with a wag of the finger.

She gaped at him.

"Consider yourself warned," he said with a grin, and exited.

Sparky gazed up at her. "I have feelings, don't I?" she asked, and the dog wagged his tail.

"Hey, Crepe," one of the guys called to Bobby. "When's your momma coming by?"

"Why would she come by?" Bobby asked.

"Doesn't she after every call?" someone else piped in.

"Yeah, since when does she need a reason?" Kenny asked, and the room broke into laughter.

Bobby shook his head. Kenny poked him in the gut, provoking a smirk. Chip kissed Fawn good-bye and then joined the men in packing equipment. A few swatted at Chip and whispered comments, undoubtedly ribbing him about Fawn.

"Chief McCabe!" Fawn called, and bounded to her. "I wanted to tell you what an honor it is that you've agreed to be one of my spiritual guides at our union ceremony. Your presence is a great blessing."

"I've been called many things, but never a blessing," Colleen said, amused.

Fawn grabbed Colleen's hand. Colleen peeked at the men, unsure what the spirited young woman was up to and afraid that her men might witness Fawn doing another reading of her aura. Once in front of Chip last summer had been bad enough.

Instead, the young woman squeezed her hand and said, "If there is anything I can ever do to repay your kindness, you just need ask."

She noticed Chip watching them and gently pulled her hand free. "Actually," she said. "There is something you can do."

"Really?" Fawn asked, delighted.

"Why don't we speak out back?" Colleen said, and walked outside with Fawn and Sparky trailing close behind.

"Everything okay?" Chip asked as they passed him.

"Just girl talk," Fawn said. She blew him a kiss.

Colleen resisted the urge to roll her eyes. One thing she had never been into was "girl talk."

"Can I ask you a question?" Fawn said as they rounded the corner to the back where the guys practiced their drills.

"Sure."

"You've got a boyfriend. What does he think of you being a firefighter?"

Colleen stopped in her tracks. There was no way she was going to discuss her relationship with Bill with Fawn. "I know you're concerned about Chip," she said. "But being a firefighter requires that he—and you—make sacrifices."

Fawn hung her head. "I worry about him."

"I know you do. And so does Chip. But there is one thing you can do to make it easier for him at the station."

"What's that?" Fawn asked, brightening.

"Try not to do your worrying here, in front of the guys. It makes it harder for Chip to do his job and gives his friends ammunition for teasing."

"No more running to the station after calls. Got it."

Colleen grinned. She could see why Chip was in love with the girl. She had a certain wonderful energy about her.

"So," Fawn said. "What is it that you wanted to ask me?"

"You and Chip live up in Carova. What's it been like up there lately?"

"How do you mean?"

"I understand there's been some tension with the tour companies," she said, wishing to remain diplomatic since she didn't know how Fawn might feel about the various factions that were in disagreement over the use of the land.

"I know the tour companies have to make a living, but there has to be a way they can do it without interfering with our animal friends."

"You mean interfering with the horses and the piping plover?"

Fawn nodded. "It's the scary Snellings and their Tour-zilla trucks that's the problem. You can't tell me those big trucks aren't doing damage."

"Why do you say the Snellings are scary?"

"Apparently, the father wanted to run his tours through someone's front yard so they could turn the tour around easier instead of using the longer route of the road. He dug into records and found out the man who owned the house had fallen on hard times and was at risk of losing his house, so he pressured the man to take money in exchange for allowing the tour to go through the property. Then the son tore up the land so badly with the truck that the man had to move out anyway. What kinda person treats people like that?"

Colleen wasn't sure if that made the Snellings scary, but they certainly sounded greedy. "What about the horse preservation society and plover foundation folks? I heard they've sometimes been at odds," she said, recalling her conversation with Myrtle.

"It's the bird people versus the horse people," Fawn said with disappointment. "My aunt Autumn is more in the piping plover camp. Personally, I think there's room for all of heaven's creatures."

Colleen wasn't surprised by this answer. Fawn's driveway was lined with adorable figurines of rabbits and chipmunks.

"You hear anything about tensions regarding construction or development?" she asked, purposely leaving out Denny's and Pinky's names, given the ongoing investigation into Denny's death.

"Nope. But if you want to know the skinny, you should talk to my aunt when she calls about having the transcendent exchange ritual."

"The what?"

"It's a ritual done at the ceremony," Fawn said. "She'll explain it all to you when you meet."

"It's not like a wedding shower, is it?" Colleen asked. She had never felt comfortable at showers—baby, wedding, or otherwise. She liked the idea of the female bonding, but had always felt like the biggest klutz in the room when she had attended past showers. She was fully aware that these events did not play to her strengths and only served to highlight how different she was from some of her sex.

Fawn giggled. "You should see your face."

"I'm sorry. I'm not good at the whole shower thing."

"There's no shower. I promise. If I know my Aunt Autumn, the ceremony won't be like anything you've been to before."

"If you say so," Colleen said, unconvinced.

"You'll see," Fawn said, and skipped off, leaving Colleen with Sparky at the back of the firehouse.

No good deed goes unpunished, she thought, and took a deep breath before heading inside. Time for an incident debriefing.

Colleen praised the men for their excellent work battling the blaze. Despite this, Chip felt bad about having left a person inside, still believing that he could have saved Denny in some way. More and more, however, she had a sinking feeling that Denny had perished before the fire and that there was nothing that her men could have done to save him—but she kept that to herself since the medical examiner's findings had not yet come back.

It had been Bobby's first big call on hoses and she commended him on the hard work he had been doing getting his weight down as well as on that day's call. After months of exercising with Chip, Bobby had almost lost enough pounds to earn his nickname Little Bobby, passed the physical tests in the fall, and earned the respect of his fellow firefighters when he had saved a boy choking on a piece of chicken by performing the Heimlich maneuver. Even Myrtle, who was usually so critical of her son, had praised his heroics. Though his mother would never say so, Colleen could see her pride every time Bobby's name was mentioned. Mother and son had come a long way.

The meeting adjourned and Colleen retreated to her office to do paperwork, answer e-mails, and write a thank-you letter to a benefactor for a generous donation he had made to the S.E.A.L.S. Ocean Safety Mini Camp for kids program. She grabbed the letter, shut down her computer, cut the lights, descended the stairs with Sparky, and dumped the letter into the outgoing mail box.

She spotted Jimmy leaning over the engine of his pickup. Time to apologize for teasing him earlier. "Hey," she said, joining him. "Everything okay?"

"Thought I heard something rattling around in here," he said, lowered the hood, and dropped it closed.

"What about with us?" she asked, genuinely concerned that she had hurt the feelings of her reliable captain.

Jimmy looked at her, puzzled for a moment, then realizing that she was referring to her earlier comment said, "Oh yeah, Cold-Hearted McCabe."

"I suppose I deserved that," she said with a smile.

"I know it's not true," he said. "But I might spread the rumor anyway."

A truck pulled in and parked next to Jimmy's pickup. Seconds later, a man with a farmer's tan, hair bleached from the sun, and wearing jeans and a light blue T-shirt exited. "Hey, Jimbo," he said and fist bumped with Jimmy. "I heard about the fire. Everyone okay?"

"We're all good," Jimmy said. "Aaron, I'd like you to meet my boss, Chief McCabe. Chief this is Aaron Lacy."

"Nice to meet you," she said.

"Aaron's the guy who started the OBX Barbecue Stand," Jimmy said.

"The food smelled wonderful today when I was driving to work," Colleen said. "I've been meaning to try it."

"Well," Aaron said, blushing slightly at the compliment. "You're going to get your chance." He popped open the cab of his truck, revealing several foil-wrapped trays. "I brought dinner for the house."

The smell of the barbecue floated toward them. "You know how to make firefighters happy," she said, her mouth salivating. "What a lovely gesture."

"It's nothing," Aaron said. "I'm just glad everyone's safe."

"Now you see why I recruited Aaron to do the cooking for tomorrow's Junior Firefighter Game Day," Jimmy said with pride. He patted his friend on the back. "Should help bring in some money."

"I hope so," Aaron said. "Care to help me transport this inside?"

They grabbed trays and made their way toward the station.

"So," Colleen said. "You started that stand a few months ago. Did you move here recently?"

"Aaron's been in Carova awhile. He's the friend I told you about that worked for Denny Custis."

"Really?" she asked, surprised. "What's that been like?"

"Why do you ask?" Aaron asked.

"Don't say anything to anyone," Jimmy said, lowering his voice. "But we think the victim in the fire was Custis."

"Wow," Aaron said. "I hadn't heard."

"We don't know for sure," Colleen quickly added. "We're waiting for an ID from the ME's office. Since you worked for him, do you know of anyone who might have had trouble with Denny?"

"Sure," Aaron said. "Practically everyone."

"Antonio Salvatore?" she asked.

"Wouldn't surprise me."

"But you hadn't heard anything specific?"

"No," the man said. "But Denny was a lousy guy to work for, particularly when it came to long hours and time off. I know it's not good to talk ill of the dead, but it's true."

"Jimmy mentioned he might have been engaging in some unorthodox zoning practices. You know anything about that?"

"I heard some of the guys did more than build houses for him. I don't know what specifically, but I didn't want any part of that. Planned on quitting as soon as I was sure I could make a go of it with this." He held up the tray of food. "Guess I'll be quitting sooner than I thought."

"Speaking of the food," Jimmy said, "we should get this inside. I'm starving."

They entered the station. The men cheered at the sight of the barbecue and everyone hurried to the tables. It was a well-deserved treat for her men and helped them end the day on a lighter note. She half listened to them chatting about the bait they used for fishing, celebrity gossip, and how they thought teams would do when football pre-season came around. Her thoughts, however, drifted to the fire and Denny's death. She didn't know how he had died, but she had every intention of finding out. Right now, however, with her belly full of food, she suddenly felt exhausted. She cleared her plate, thanked Aaron for the meal, said good-bye to her guys, and headed home with Sparky for a shower and a good night's sleep.

Chapter 7

Colleen felt warm breath blow across her forehead and the soft, cool pad of a paw gently pat her cheek. She fought to keep her face still and her lids from fluttering, but it was no use. Smokey knew she was awake, purred loudly in her ear, and rubbed her furry head against Colleen's chin. A cat wanting breakfast is better than an alarm clock.

"Hey there," Colleen said, finally opening her eyes and rubbing the Siamese's cheek. "Why can't you be like Sparky and let me sleep?"

Smokey replied with an insistent meow, jumped from the bed, ran to the door, curved back, and meowed again.

"Okay okay," she said. She climbed out of bed and made her way downstairs, trying all the while not to trip as Smokey darted between her legs.

Sparky wagged his tail and Colleen opened the front door to

let him out to take care of business. She yawned and stretched from side to side before preparing Smokey's breakfast and pouring food into Sparky's bowl. Nothing like the smell of canned cat food in the morning, she thought, and wrinkled her nose. Sparky pawed at the front screen and she let him in.

Truthfully, she didn't mind Smokey's approach to waking her in the morning. It sure beat the irritating buzz of her alarm clock. She retrieved a bottle of vitamin water from the refrigerator and gulped it down so she'd be hydrated for her run. She checked the time. It would be early enough for a nice leisurely jog.

She dashed upstairs, washed her face, brushed her teeth, threw on her running gear, and rejoined Sparky, who was waiting by the front door with his leash in his mouth. She stroked Smokey's back and headed out into the misty early morning. She strolled to the end of her driveway and stretched her legs. Sparky looked at her as if to say "You ready?" and they set off on Lakeview Court toward Route 12.

Running had always helped clear her mind. Right now there was quite a bit swirling around in there—Denny's and Fuentes's deaths, Agent Morgan and the arson investigation, Fawn and Chip's wedding, the disguised Myrtle and her battles over the use of the sanctuary land, and Denny and Pinky's feud.

She wondered if she'd hear from Agent Morgan today about any findings. More and more she suspected that Denny had been the one that had set the fire. Why else would he have been on Pinky's property? Perhaps he hadn't expected the place to burn so fast and, with his poor vision and the billowing smoke, had had trouble finding his way out. Too many times people died in fires because they couldn't see their way to an exit.

And what about the man that had been seen arguing with Denny before the fire? Was it possible this person had killed Denny and his employee Michael Fuentes? Perhaps the first death had been a warning to Denny from an enemy—the developer had certainly made a few. But who hated him enough to kill him and, perhaps, one of his crew?

She approached Route 12 and made a right toward Currituck Heritage Park. The park was home to the Currituck Beach Lighthouse, the Whalehead historic house and museum, and the Outer Banks Center for Wildlife Education and was one of her favorite places in Corolla. Her phone vibrated in her armband. She slipped it from its pocket and glanced at the number.

"Good morning," she said after hitting the ANSWER button.

"You're up already?" Bill asked, surprised.

"Smokey."

"Ah," he said.

"What's up?"

"ME called with preliminary findings on Custis. No soot or ash in his airways and a fracture at the back of his skull. Looks like we've got a—"

"Homicide," Colleen said with him, and tapped Sparky's rump to signal him to stop.

"I'm on my way to pick up Salvatore."

"You're arresting Pinky?"

"Not yet," he said. "But I'd like to question him, see where he was yesterday."

She understood why Bill wanted to speak with Pinky. The real estate developer had been evasive about where he had been when the fire broke out, had been involved in recent disputes over land with the victim, and owned the property where Denny had died; but Colleen didn't believe for a minute that Pinky was responsible for the fire or the death.

"You there?" Bill asked.

"Yep." She looked north up Route 12 and got an idea.

"I gotta go," Bill said. "Thought you'd want to know."

"Thanks. Keep me posted," she said, and jogged north instead of south along Route 12.

There's no way Pinky killed Denny, she thought. She picked up her pace, checked for traffic, crossed Route 12, turned onto Headwind Way and then onto Sandcastle Drive. Time to return to the scene of the crime.

She slowed upon reaching the remains of Pinky's construction site. Sparky cocked his head and his nostrils twitched. He had an especially sensitive nose when it came to fire. He whimpered to be let free and she unhooked his leash. It wouldn't hurt to have a canine detective on the case. He sniffed at the ground and the pylons holding up the house, then zigzagged toward the back. She ducked under the crime-scene tape and stared up at the charred building.

Burned structures always came across as angry to her with their jagged edges, tarnished and twisted metal, and crusty blackness that covered everything. She walked around the side, examined the V-shaped burn marks coming from the window, and continued to the ocean side of the house. Sparky burrowed his nose into the sand near where they had found the matches and scratched the ground with his paws. She backed away until she reached the foot of the dune. Maybe getting a different perspective would help her figure out what had happened here.

Sparky barked and she searched for him on the property.

"Bring me the ball," came a boy's voice from behind a dune that stood between the neighboring house and Pinky's property. A ball flew high into the air on the other side of the dune, fell back to earth, and was followed by a "Good dog."

She trudged up the sand berm and caught sight of Sparky playing with the boy who had witnessed Denny arguing with the mystery man. "Hello," she said. "I see you've met Sparky."

Sparky licked the boy's face. The boy laughed and said, "Stop that, Sparky."

Colleen beamed. Sparky had always had a way with children. She carefully made her way down the other side and onto a manicured backyard complete with hot tub, badminton net, and shuffleboard.

"I'm Colleen," she said. "What's your name?"

"Jacob."

"Nice to meet you, Jacob. Do you remember me from yesterday?"

The boy looked at her puzzled and then his face brightened. "You're the lady firefighter. I like your engine."

"Everyone does." She hadn't met a child yet that didn't love seeing the inside of the engine and ambulance.

"Jacob?" came a woman's voice from above them. "Who are you talking to?"

"The lady firefighter. She's got a dog!"

The boy's mother hurried down the stairs and joined them. "Is there a problem?" she asked.

Colleen held out her hand. "I'm Chief McCabe. I understand Jacob witnessed an argument yesterday before the fire."

"That's right," Jacob's mother said.

"I was wondering if I might ask him a few questions, to help me better understand the circumstances surrounding the incident."

"You okay with that?" the mother asked her son.

"Sure."

Colleen squatted next to Jacob so they were at the same level. "You mind telling me everything you heard or saw? Even if you don't think it's important, it might help me figure out how that fire started."

"Is Sparky a firehouse dog?" Jacob asked, stroking the dog's neck.

"Kinda," Colleen said, wanting him to get to her question but not wishing to rush him. "But he lives with me, not at the station."

"That's cool."

"Jacob, tell Chief McCabe what you saw," the mother said.

"Well," he said in a tone that indicated he was about to tell a long, once-upon-a-time story. "It all began with a lot of banging around."

"What type of banging?" Colleen asked.

"I don't know. Banging like when people build stuff."

"Construction noise?"

"Kinda."

"Okay," Colleen said. "What then?"

"I looked out my window and this weird-looking man came in a pickup and parked next to the white truck. Then another man came out of the house and started fighting with the weird-looking man . . . but nobody hit anybody or anything. They were just fighting with words."

"Could you hear what they were saying?"

Jacob shook his head.

"What happened after that?"

"I went to get my mom but when we looked out the window again the weird man was driving away and the other man was gone."

Colleen glanced at the mother. "Did you see the man in the pickup?"

"Not really. Dark hair was all I could make out."

"This is important," Colleen said, turning back to Jacob. "Try to think really hard. Is there anything about the weird man that you can remember? Maybe what he was wearing or how tall he was?"

"He was pretty short, maybe like mom's size, and he wore this big orange shirt. Oh, and he had strange hair—like a helmet or something."

Colleen's jaw clenched. "Did he have any facial hair, a beard or moustache or maybe sideburns?"

"What are sideburns?" he asked with interest.

"Like Daddy has here," the mother said, indicating the sides of her cheeks.

Jacob pursed his lips, thinking, and nodded. "But they were much bigger than Daddy's."

Colleen silently groaned. The weird-looking man could only be one person . . . Myrtle Crepe. What had her former teacher done?

"Does that help?" the boy's mother asked, ready to take Jacob back inside.

"Very much," she said. "We're having a game day at the station this afternoon, Jacob. If you come by, we'll have a special junior firefighter badge for you."

"Can I see the fire engine, too?" he asked, his eyes widening with awe.

"And the ambulance if you'd like."

Jacob hopped up and dashed to his mother. "Can we go to the station now?"

"Why don't we have breakfast first," his mother said and rubbed his head.

"The badge will be there whenever you're ready," Colleen said, noticing Jacob's disappointed expression.

He beamed. "I can't wait to tell Dad. See you at the fire station, Sparky," he said, gave Sparky a hug, and ran inside yelling "Dad!"

"I should go," Colleen said, leashing Sparky. "Thank you for letting me speak with your son. He's a smart kid."

"Good luck with figuring out what started that fire."

"Thanks. Come on," she said to Sparky, and the two climbed the berm.

She scratched Sparky's ears when they reached the other side. The dog had more than earned a treat for his help with the boy. She walked under the house where the carport would have been and then it hit her. Jacob had reported seeing two vehicles—one that belonged to the man that Colleen now realized had been Myrtle in disguise and one that belonged to Denny. When they had arrived on the scene, however, Denny's pickup was gone. What had happened to it? Had it been stolen or moved by the killer?

She'd bet anything that Denny's keys had not been found on his person. If that proved true, then it was possible that whoever had murdered Denny had driven off with his truck. If they could find the truck, it might contain evidence that could lead them to his killer.

She removed her phone from her armband, hit speed dial, and got Bill's voice mail. "Bill, I have new information about the case. Give me a call as soon as you get this." She hung up. What she had learned from the boy could help clear Pinky . . . or land Myrtle in jail.

Chapter 8

How do you tell your beau the sheriff that your sexagenarian former third-grade teacher turned horse preservationist has been dressing up as fat Elvis, spying on a homicide victim, and was the last person to see that person alive, without making her a suspect?

Colleen sat in her idling SUV in a shady spot of the Sheriff's Department parking lot. She had left Sparky at home—something she rarely did. After the morning jog, he had fallen asleep in the living room while she got ready. When she had called for him to leave with her, he had opened his eyes and then closed them again. She hadn't had the heart to force him from his bed. He had earned a day of rest after the good work he had done with the boy. She had also called Jimmy to let him know she might be a few minutes late as there had been new developments in the case. Colleen had been sitting in her vehicle for the better part of ten minutes mulling over how to tell Bill about Myrtle without getting Myrtle in trouble and had come up empty. Every time she ran through an explanation of what Myrtle had been up to it sounded crazy.

She noted the time. The longer she sat in the parking lot, the longer Pinky sat in the holding area. Maybe inspiration will come to me when I see Bill, she thought as she exited the SUV and then entered the Sheriff's Department. She spotted Rodney near the interview rooms at the end of the hall.

"Hey, Rodney," she said, approaching the deputy.

"Hey."

"I left Bill a message. Found out information that might be helpful to the case."

"He's in with Salvatore," the deputy said, and motioned to a room labeled INTERVIEW ROOM 2.

"How's it going?" she asked, wishing she had X-ray vision and super hearing.

Rodney moved a short distance away from the door and lowered his voice. "Salvatore insists he knows nothing about what happened with Custis."

"I don't think he does," she whispered back, and Rodney gave a slight nod. "You don't seem surprised."

"It's not that . . ."

Bill's absence on the homeland security detail had afforded her the opportunity to become further acquainted with Rodney, and the more time she had spent with Bill's deputy, the better she had liked him. She had also learned to read him and sensed now there was something he wasn't telling her. She recalled his comment about Denny on the beach when they had discovered Fuentes' body.

"You never cared for Custis," she said.

Before he could answer, Bill emerged from the interrogation room and ran his hands through his hair. "Hello," he said, surprised to see her.

"Did you get my message?" she asked.

"I've been in with Salvatore. Was it something important?"

"I spoke with the kid—the one who saw a man arguing with Custis."

Bill raised a brow. "When was this?"

She resisted the urge to roll her eyes. Why did he always get on her about getting involved in cases?

Rodney observed the two. "Maybe I should go."

She touched his arm to stop him. "After you called," she said to Bill. "I jogged by the house to see if I had missed anything or could find a clue as to what had occurred there."

"Okay," Bill said. "But how did you end up speaking with the boy?"

"Sparky wandered next door and when I retrieved him he was playing with the boy. I think I know who the boy saw arguing with Denny, but I don't think he is a he. I think he's a she, but not our guy or gal or—"

"Stop," Bill said. "Do you know what she's talking about?" he asked Rodney.

"This is the first I'm hearing any of this."

"Are you saying you think the person seen arguing with Custis was a woman?" Bill asked.

"Yes."

"Even though everyone, including our young witness, said they saw a man?"

"You're missing the point," she said. "I don't think Pinky's the killer."

"You think it's this woman," Rodney said.

"No. I don't think that person's the killer either."

"Who's the woman?" Bill asked, losing patience.

Bill and Rodney waited. If she said the name then Bill would almost certainly bring Myrtle in. And if she didn't, Pinky would be blamed for something he didn't do. She took a deep breath, hesitated, and then said, "Myrtle."

Several seconds of stunned silence passed before Bill said, "Myrtle Crepe?"

"Apparently, she's been disguising herself—rather badly I might add—as a man."

"Why would Mrs. Crepe dress like a man?" Rodney asked, baffled.

Colleen and Bill locked eyes. The two were familiar with another occasion when Myrtle had disguised herself as a man in order to go "undercover."

"She was trying to catch Denny in the act of interfering with the horses," she said.

Rodney scratched his head. "But there aren't any horses in that area."

"I'm sure she was confronting him about it."

Bill stared at her intently. She hated when he cast that look on her. She could see why he had a reputation for getting suspects to confess to their crimes.

"How'd you know the boy's description of the man was Myrtle in disguise?"

She had been hoping to avoid it, but she was going to have to explain it all if she had any expectation of getting Bill to understand. "Because she drove by Denny's place Saturday when I was there. Denny said she had been stalking him, doing drive-bys. You know, he had really terrible vision."

"He must, to think Mrs. Crepe was a man," Rodney said.

"So why shouldn't I bring Myrtle in?" Bill asked.

"Because I think it's entirely possible that someone else was in the house."

Bill threw up his hands and walked away. She understood his frustration. If she was right, it meant they were no closer to catching the murderer than they had been the day before.

Rodney noted her worried expression. "Give him a second. He'll be back."

True to his deputy's word, Bill returned a moment later. "Okay. Let me hear why you think there was a third person at the house. Then I'll decide whether we cut Salvatore loose and arrest Myrtle Crepe."

Colleen remembered when Myrtle used to get on her when she was a student about not knowing how to cut to the chase with a story. Better keep it short and sweet, she thought. Pinky—and Myrtle's—freedom depended on it.

"Jacob, that's the boy, told me he saw two vehicles—Myrtle's truck and another, presumably Denny's. But there weren't any vehicles at the scene when we arrived."

"Which means someone moved it," Rodney said.

"Or that Salvatore drove it away," Bill said. "It could have been his truck."

"Then how did Denny get there?" she asked. "Denny didn't seem like someone into long walks on the beach." Bill would have to admit, it was unlikely Denny had arrived on foot. "Did the ME find any keys on Denny's body?"

"No," Bill said.

"Isn't that strange that Denny didn't have any keys, even house keys, with him?"

"Maybe somebody took them and the truck," Rodney said.

"Or," Bill said, "Salvatore lured Denny there and then drove away in his own car."

"Only one way to find out," Colleen said.

They'd have to ask Pinky.

"Go ahead and pick up Myrtle," Bill said to Rodney, and turned to enter the interrogation room.

"Really?" Rodney asked, then saw that Bill was serious. "Right," he said, and departed to pick up Myrtle.

"Why not wait to bring Myrtle in?" she asked. "At least until we hear what Pinky has to say?"

"She was at the scene. If she doesn't have anything to hide then we'll find that out and let her go."

"But—" she protested.

"And, if your theory of a third man is correct, she might have observed something while she was speaking with Denny."

She couldn't argue with that. "I hate when you're right."

He grinned and reached for the interrogation room doorknob.

"Bill, wait," she said, grabbing his hand. "Why not let me come in?"

"Why would I do that?" he asked. "You got a thing for Salvatore?"

"No," she said. Sometimes Bill could be such a guy. "But he trusts me."

"You mean likes you."

"If that's true, you might get more out of him if I'm in there."

He studied her. She had no idea if he'd go for it or not. Chances were fifty-fifty. "Okay," he finally said, and opened the door.

"Chief McCabe," Pinky said as they entered. "What a nice surprise. Have you come to bust me out of here?"

She smiled, caught Bill frowning at her, and her smile swiftly disappeared. She and Bill sat across a round table from Pinky, who sat in a chair in the corner. It was a common interrogation technique to position a suspect in a corner. The position made those being questioned uncomfortable and investigators often increased the pressure by sitting within a suspect's personal space. Bill sat opposite Pinky. She took a chair to the side.

"Chief McCabe has brought some information to my attention," Bill said. Pinky viewed her quizzically. "We have a witness who spotted one of your construction trucks at the house the morning of the fire."

"That's impossible," Pinky said.

"And why is that?" Bill asked, leaning back and writing on a notepad.

"My men don't work on Sunday."

"What about you?"

"I'm Catholic," Pinky said with pride. "Sundays are a day to be with one's family, attend mass, reflect on how fortunate we are. I know it may sound old-fashioned but that's how I was raised."

"So that's where you were Sunday morning?" Bill asked, skeptical. "At church services?"

Pinky straightened in his chair. Colleen believed that Pinky hadn't been at the house that morning, but why was he so reluctant to tell them where he was?

"If you tell us," she said. "Bill can verify your story and you can be out of here."

"I'm afraid I can't do that."

"You sure you didn't lure Custis there?" Bill asked. "If what you say is true, you knew you wouldn't be disturbed by your men."

"First, I would never invite that man onto my property. Second, everyone in this business is well aware of my Sundays-off policy . . . including Mr. Custis. As I said before, I wouldn't be surprised if he went there to vandalize my project."

"But nobody can corroborate that or your story, can they?" Bill said, putting the notepad down.

Pinky didn't answer. Colleen wanted to shake him. Didn't he realize he could go to jail for murder? What would make him put everything at risk? Then it hit her. Only one thing could make Pinky stay quiet . . . a woman. She wondered if it had been such a good idea for her to be in the room. Given his past flirtations, maybe he was reluctant to reveal the woman's identity.

"Who is she?" Colleen asked.

Bill's cheeks flushed pink. She knew he would misunderstand

the question—think she was asking it out of jealousy—but she didn't care. Pinky was being stubborn. Pinky locked eyes with her and she knew in an instant she was correct. He was protecting a woman . . . who she was or why, she didn't know.

"I'm sorry," Pinky said with sincerity.

"Bill will be discreet," she said. "Won't you?"

The tension in Bill's jaw diminished at the revelation that Pinky may have been with a lady friend.

"Save your breath, Sheriff," Pinky said before Bill could reassure Pinky about his discretion. "I don't know anything else." And with that Pinky sat back in his chair and folded his arms.

That was it. Pinky wasn't going to reveal the identity of his paramour. Bill rose and she followed him to the door.

"Let us know if you change your mind," she said, stealing a glance back at Pinky.

"You'll be the first," he said with a wink.

She smiled and exited the room. "So?" she said to Bill as they walked down the hall toward his office. "What do you think?"

"We'll see what happens when Rodney brings Myrtle in. In the meantime, Salvatore stays."

"You really don't believe Myrtle killed someone, do you?" He didn't respond. "Do you?"

"I can't imagine how Myrtle would overcome a man of Denny's size, but you never know."

She checked her watch. She had been hoping to stick around and do some damage control when Myrtle arrived, but she was due at the station for the kid's firefighter game day. The phone on Bill's desk rang. He crossed into his office and picked up.

"Dorman," he said and listened. "Did you try the preservation society office? . . . Okay, then. Let me know when you find her." Bill hung up. "Rodney's still searching for Myrtle."

"I should get going," she said. Bill escorted her to the front door of the Sheriff's Department building. "We'll be busy at the station, but keep me posted about Myrtle."

She exited and crossed to her SUV, thankful that, given the soaring temperature, it was parked in the shade of the pine trees that lined the side of the building. She pulled out and drove south on Route 12. She had traveled about a mile when something sharp suddenly poked her in her right side.

"Don't move," came a muffled voice from the backseat.

Colleen froze, stunned by the presence of an intruder.

"Keep driving," the voice ordered.

Her eyes narrowed. There was something familiar about that voice. She squeezed the steering wheel in exasperation. "Myrtle!"

Colleen felt what she now realized were fingers ease up on her side, then push against her again. "I'm not Myrtle," said the intruder.

"Okay, person-who-is-not-Myrtle," Colleen said, now certain it was indeed her former teacher, "You mind telling me what you're doing hiding in my backseat with two fingers to my side?"

"I'm on the lam."

She bit her lip to keep from laughing and stretched to see if she could see Myrtle in her rearview mirror. "You know, everyone is looking for you."

"So I heard on the police scanner."

Colleen slowed and pulled off on a side street to turn around. "I'm taking you back to the Sheriff's Department."

Myrtle poked her hard in the side.

"Hey," Colleen said. "Ease up on those boney fingers."

"You can't take me in," Myrtle said, popping up from the backseat and leaning forward.

"Watch me," she said, getting back onto Route 12.

"Please," Myrtle said. "There's a foal that might be in trouble."

"What are you talking about?"

"Someone reported that they thought our new foal was lame—traveling on the tips of her hooves—which could mean she has contracted tendons. If not corrected, the foal could end up crippled. I won't know if the report is accurate until I see her."

Colleen sighed. She admired Myrtle's passion for the welfare of the horses, but right now there was also the important matter of murder. "Couldn't Nellie or the herd manager do it?"

"Please," Myrtle begged. "Time is critical. She could be in need of rescue."

Before Colleen had a chance to tell Myrtle she'd take her to the sanctuary, Myrtle flung open the back door and said, "Forget it."

"Myrtle! Close that door!" she yelled, fearful that the woman would leap from the moving vehicle.

Myrtle struggled with the door and then slammed it closed. "So you'll help me?"

"If I do, you'll turn yourself in to the sheriff?"

"Absolutely," Myrtle said, then ducked down in the backseat as they passed the Sheriff's Department building.

Colleen shook her head and sped up Route 12 to Carova to check on the foal with Myrtle. Bill's going to hate this, she thought.

Chapter 9

"There's nothing more beautiful than seeing a horse free and in its natural habitat," Myrtle said, staring through binoculars down a narrow trail that cut through the marshy foliage of the refuge.

Yes, Colleen thought, and the sooner we see the foal and make sure she's healthy, the sooner I can take you to the Sheriff's Department. It wasn't that she didn't share Myrtle's love of the horses. She did. They were truly magnificent creatures; but right now Colleen felt a little like she was aiding and abetting a criminal.

"You sure they're up here?" Colleen asked. They had been waiting in this spot with the engine off for twenty minutes and, despite the breeze coming through the open windows, the heat inside the SUV was oppressive.

Before Myrtle could answer, a large monster of a tour vehicle rumbled over a nearby dune. Tour-zilla was one of a number of local companies that gave horse tours, and was famous for its vibrant green trucks with enormous Godzilla-type heads attached to the fronts, lizard scales painted on the sides, and reptile-type tails hanging from the backs. Colleen caught a brief glimpse of the tattooed driver as the truck wobbled past them with an open back full of sunburned tourists and then disappeared around a bend in the sandy road leaving a section of squashed shrubs and deep tire tracks in its wake.

"Snelling," Myrtle hissed with disgust.

Colleen's brows raised in surprise at the sudden outburst.

"The Snellings have made millions off of the horses with that Tour-zilla company and have never given one cent to help them. Did you know that?"

"No." Colleen had to admit, there was something wrong about their lack of support, especially since their business depended on the horses thriving. Apparently, the people living in Carova weren't the only ones subject to the Snellings' disrespect.

"They wanted to drive a bus even larger than that truck through here. Can you imagine the damage something bigger would do? The piping plover folks and I took it to the state legislature, got them to cap the vehicle size."

The bushes rustled and moments later a horse emerged. Colleen held her breath.

"Not her. The foal's mother has a blaze," Myrtle said referring to the horse's nose markings.

Two more horses emerged from the brush, blinked lazily at them, and munched on leaves.

"That's Lightning, Bella, and Gonzalo," Myrtle said, pointing to each.

"How can you tell them apart?" she asked, studying them.

"Some have socks," Myrtle said, indicating the white on one of the horse's hooves, "The markings on the nose, how their mane falls to one side or the other . . . It's not hard."

She had to hand it to Myrtle: she may rub people the wrong way, but there wasn't a person on the planet more dedicated to Corolla's horses. She wasn't surprised Myrtle had gone to the North Carolina legislature, but she was surprised that those protecting the piping plover had cooperated with her.

"I thought you weren't too fond of the piping plover folks," Colleen said, wiping sweat from her temple and upper lip and watching the horses move down the trail, tails swishing.

"Who told you that?"

"Don't they blame the horses for destroying the plover's nests?"

"Poppycock," Myrtle said. "That rumor was started by the duck hunters because they were worried they'd be restricted from hunting on the property. Nothing with legs is destroying those nests. It's those monster wheels that are doing it."

Colleen checked the time. It was getting late. As much as she hated to abandon their mission, Myrtle would have to search for the foal later. "I'm afraid the stakeout's over," she said, reaching for the keys in the ignition. She glanced in her rearview mirror and froze. Standing a short distance behind the SUV was a stunning chestnut with a white stripe down her nose nudging a furry foal. "Myrtle," she whispered and pointed out the back window.

Myrtle twisted in her seat. "That's her."

"She's beautiful," Colleen said in awe.

The two quietly observed mother and offspring nuzzling one another. The mare shook her mane and it billowed in the ocean air. The foal bounced across the road, healthy and happy. Myrtle smiled with pride and Colleen sighed with relief. The mare led the foal across the trail and then both disappeared behind a dune. If I get flack for not bringing Myrtle in right away, Colleen thought, it was well worth it.

"You good now?" she asked.

"Take me in, Chief."

She started the engine, blasted the air conditioning, adjusted a vent so the air hit her straight in the face, and rolled up the windows.

"I'll text them that we're coming," she said.

Colleen texted first Bill and then Rodney that she had Myrtle in Carova. Seconds later a text came back from Rodney that he was already in Carova and would pick Myrtle up himself. She agreed to meet Rodney at the nearest access point.

"Deputy Warren is picking you up," Colleen said. "When they question you I want you to tell them everything: why you've been in that silly disguise, how long you've been stalking Denny, how you found him at Pinky's house, and anything you noticed yesterday when you confronted him."

"I'll do my best," Myrtle said, barely paying attention.

She stole a look at Myrtle as she steered around a pool of water. "You better or you could be arrested."

"Fiddledeedee."

She wanted to scream. In all her life she'd never known anyone as annoying as Myrtle. "Do you want to be charged with murder?"

"Murder?" Myrtle said, taken aback. "I thought it was an arson investigation."

Shoot. She had said too much. "It's both."

"Denny Custis was murdered?"

"How did you know it was Denny?" Colleen asked.

"Corolla's small. Heard a rumor it was Custis in that fire, but I hadn't heard it was murder."

"Now do you see why you need to be completely honest with the sheriff?" Myrtle stared out the side window. "What were you doing there, anyway?"

Myrtle said nothing. Better to let Bill question her anyway. They drove the rest of the way to the rendezvous in silence. When they arrived, Rodney was waiting for them.

"You ready?" she asked Myrtle as she stopped.

"No problem," Myrtle said. She exited and trekked toward Rodney with her wrists thrust out in front of her ready to be handcuffed.

Rodney waved Myrtle's hands away. She hoped Myrtle treated the questioning seriously and told Bill everything. Rodney took Myrtle by the arm, helped her into his pickup, walked around the back, gave Colleen a quick wave, slid into the driver's side, and drove away with Myrtle—currently Corolla's Most Wanted.

Colleen pushed tendrils of hair from her face. She felt sticky and wanted to wash her hands. Suddenly, there was a tap at the driver's side window. She startled, then discovered an attractive woman in her early forties smiling at her. She rolled down the window.

"What can I do for you?" Colleen asked.

"I'm glad I saw you. I've been looking forward to meeting you," the woman said.

"You sure you don't have me confused with someone else?"

"I'm Autumn Harkins, Fawn's aunt," the woman said, and held out her hand.

"Of course."

She shook Autumn's hand and noted roses and sunflowers tattooed like rings around several of her fingers.

"I'm sorry you had a hard time finding the place. Fawn didn't tell me you were coming."

"Well, actually—" Colleen said, attempting to interrupt.

"I can't wait to tell you about the ceremony."

"I think there's a bit of a misunderstanding. Not that it isn't lovely to meet you, but I'm overdue at the station." She knew Jimmy would have the Junior Firefighter's Game Day under control but wanted to get back to meet with visitors.

Autumn smirked. "Fawn and Chip warned me you'd be elusive. A fear of commitment perhaps?"

"No, I really do—"

"Relax. I think you're wise not to jump into anything too fast. Although I wouldn't wait too long. That sheriff could give George Clooney a run for his money. It's a wonder someone hasn't nabbed him already."

Colleen silently groaned. Even complete strangers were apparently aware of her romantic life. Please don't let her read my aura or tea leaves or whatever mystical thing she might be into, she prayed.

"Don't worry, I promise not to read your aura," the woman said knowingly. "You look like you've been out in the heat awhile. Sure you don't want to come in and have a cool drink?"

"I really must go."

Autumn placed a hand on her hip and gave Colleen a sideways glance. "The wedding *is* this weekend. I've done all the work. Fawn just needs to know you've signed off on it."

"Okay okay," she said. Better to get this over with and get on with her day. "Where do you live?"

"Over there," she said, indicating a blue house fifteen yards beyond a nearby dune. "I'll meet you." And with that Autumn vanished along a narrow trail between the dunes as suddenly as she had appeared.

Chapter 10

Colleen alighted from her SUV and stared in wonder at Autumn's yard. Arranged in various positions as if reclining, frolicking, or climbing the dunes, were a Who's Who of rock-and-roll molded celebrity statues. Buddy Holly sported his signature black-rimmed glasses and strummed a banjo; Jimi Hendrix huddled over his guitar at the top of a dune; and Madonna lounged seductively on her side in a leather corset, grass growing around her like a halo.

"You like them?" Autumn called from a second-floor deck.

"They're quite good," Colleen said, taking in the dozen or so statues as she approached the house. "You did all of these?"

"Yep. I'm doing Sonny and Cher for Fawn and Chip. They love 'I Got You Babe.' But don't say anything. It's a surprise."

She caught sight of a statue tucked to the side of the house, not yet painted and glazed. The face was familiar, but she had a hard time deciphering what celebrity it would eventually be. Maybe when the artist was finished she'd be able to tell.

"Welcome to my oasis," Autumn said, holding open the screen door.

She was surprised to discover the interior of Autumn's modest house looking more like an art gallery than a beach getaway. Recessed lighting shined on eggshell-white walls lined with carefully arranged portraits of music legends, politicians, actors, and poets. The paintings were vibrant, like their subjects, and the splashes of color gave the images an almost wild movement. Underscoring the gallery-like appearance were sparse furnishings—two contemporary floor lamps with white shades, a large teak coffee table surrounded by sleek beige leather chairs, and a simple bamboo rug.

"Too art gallery?" Autumn asked, observing Colleen.

"No," she said. "It's nice. Although I don't feel like I can touch anything."

"Don't be ridiculous. If something happens, I can just slap more paint on it," Autumn said with an easy laugh, and disappeared through a doorway.

Colleen was pleasantly surprised by Fawn's aunt. Maybe discussing the wedding with the woman wouldn't be so bad after all. She followed the artist into a room that served as a combined kitchen, dining, and living room with floor-to-ceiling glass windows that overlooked the top of the dunes and ocean. This area was much more like what she had expected: an easel with paints faced the ocean, the dining table was covered in newspaper and modeling clay, and crystals hanging in front of windows sparkled brightly in the breeze.

"Would you like some iced tea?" Autumn asked. "I just made a pitcher."

"I'm fine."

"You sure? I didn't flavor it with anything exotic."

She wasn't sure what Autumn meant by "exotic," but it did reassure her. "Iced tea sounds great."

Autumn hummed and poured two glasses.

"You were on TV," Colleen said, suddenly recognizing Autumn as the artist she saw interviewed the other night as she fell asleep.

"That's me."

"I see you like Halloween," Colleen said, noticing a piece of driftwood decorated with pumpkin, black cat, and ghost ornaments.

"I should have been born then," she said with a wicked smile.

"Why? Are you a witch?" Colleen asked with a chuckle.

"According to my ex."

"I'm sorry," Colleen said, now embarrassed by her comment.

"Don't be. I've been separated almost two years. He was the biggest mistake of my life. Went back to my maiden name. Never confuse jealousy and anger for passion," she said, and raised her glass for emphasis.

Uncomfortable with the personal nature of their conversation, Colleen took a sip of the iced tea. It was flavored with a hint of mint—and unexpectedly delicious. She guzzled half the glass.

"I heard about the fire," Autumn said, refilling Colleen's glass. "Such a shame. That house had lovely views."

"You've been inside?" Colleen asked.

Autumn averted eye contact and crossed to the window. "Speaking of lovely views," she said, ignoring Colleen's question, "I was thinking we might have the rehearsal dinner down there." She pointed to a cozy area between the house and frontal dune.

Colleen noted tension in Autumn's posture that hadn't been there seconds ago. Why had her question caused such a reaction? And why had the artist refused to answer it? Had she offended her in some way? Or was it something else? She glanced around the room—now uneasy herself—and noted containers of mineral spirits, linseed oil, and turpentine in a corner by an open window—substances known for their use with paints. But they were also known for their toxic vapors and flammability. She studied Autumn staring out the window. Was it possible Fawn's aunt was their arsonist? The instant the question popped into her head, she knew it was rash. Just because the woman was in possession of an accelerant or two didn't mean she was a criminal. Then again, the woman had already admitted to having been at the house on at least one occasion. Stop! she scolded herself. Why are you jumping to conclusions about this woman? Sometimes paint supplies are just paint supplies. You can't go around suspecting everyone you meet of arson or murder. Besides, the artist hardly fits the usual profile of an arsonist.

Despite knowing it was irrational to suspect the woman simply because she was in possession of art supplies, Colleen couldn't help herself from pursuing the idea. "Do you paint in the morning?" she asked, trying to appear as if making small talk.

"Sometimes," Autumn said.

"Is that what you were doing Sunday morning?"

"Actually," the artist said, facing her, "I was having breakfast with a friend."

"If you don't mind my asking . . . who?" It was rather presumptuous to pose such a personal question to a stranger, but Colleen was willing to risk being rude if it was in service to public safety.

"I'm afraid that's rather private."

Why was everyone being so secretive lately? She studied Autumn again with a new theory. The artist was striking, with flowing auburn hair, porcelain skin, and deep blue eyes. Colleen imagined that she had attracted more than a few admirers. Perhaps she was with a man and, given the pending nature of her divorce, didn't want anyone to know.

"Is something wrong?" Autumn asked.

Colleen's cheeks flushed pink, realizing she had been staring at the woman. "I don't mean to pry. I know we've just met, but would you mind telling me how you know about the inside of the house? It's important."

Autumn relaxed. "Fawn was right about your aura. Definitely pink."

"I guess pink is my color," she said, trying to make a joke of what had been an embarrassing occasion last summer when Fawn had done a reading.

"Antonio—Mr. Salvatore—hired me to paint a mural on one of the walls. I met him there a few weeks ago to see the space so I'd know what I'd be working with."

"And how do you know Mr. Salvatore?"

"He's commissioned a few works, mostly fountains or statues, for his relatives up north. He has quite an eye for art," she said with admiration. "Any other questions, Inspector?"

Despite the friendly tone of the question, Colleen got the message. She was being nosey.

"One more," she said. "Living up here, did you ever have any dealings with Denny Custis?"

"Thank goodness, no."

"I take it from your reaction that you're not a fan."

"He has no regard for the plover nests. A few weeks ago we found one on his property and had it fenced off for protection. Somehow that fencing mysteriously disappeared."

"You think he removed it?" Colleen asked with concern. The piping plover was an endangered species. It was against the law to disturb their nests.

"I think that man got exactly what he deserved," she said. "And I'm not sorry to say it."

"I see you've heard the news," Colleen said. She was stunned by the intensity of Autumn's reaction. Could it be that her suspicions about Autumn being the arsonist weren't so crazy after all?

"You must have a lot to do," the artist said, changing the subject and grabbing a notebook. "I'd best get to showing you what I have in mind for the ceremony."

For the next twenty minutes, Autumn reviewed the plans for the wedding. Colleen only half listened as Autumn discussed the colors, fabrics, and something about bringing a love quote to the ceremony. It wasn't until Autumn started discussing the flowers and bouquet that Colleen perked up. There was something about the way she spoke about the flowers that sounded familiar . . . like Colleen had heard the explanation of the flowers' meanings before. Then it struck her . . . Pinky. He had told Colleen last summer about how his mother had run a florist shop and explained the meanings of several different flowers. Did Autumn's relationship with Pinky go beyond art commissions? Was it possible Autumn was the person Pinky was protecting by refusing to tell Bill his whereabouts on the morning of the fire? Or was it the other way around? Was Autumn protecting Pinky?

She pushed the questions from her mind and focused on the upcoming nuptials. Autumn moved on to the attire and—much to Colleen's relief and true to Fawn's word—Autumn suggested Colleen wear whatever she felt suited the occasion. "This day is all about helping celebrate Fawn and Chip's union," she had said. "Anything that distracts us from that—such as feeling uncomfortable in a dress, for example—is unwelcome."

She left Fawn's aunt with her to-do list, proud that she had survived the wedding plan conference and armed with new information. She started her SUV, eager to be back at the station and in her element, and was about to pull away when Autumn came running down the stairs toward her.

"I almost forgot," Autumn said, catching her breath, and held out her hand through the open driver's-side window. "This is for you."

Colleen took a small velvet pouch. "What is it?"

"Open it," Autumn said.

She untied the pouch and out rolled a hexagon-cut pink crystal on a silver ribbon. "Thank you," she said, stunned by the gift.

"You don't have to wear it, but I thought you might like a little something special for the wedding." Autumn gave her a wink, swiveled, and sashayed away.

She glanced at the necklace in her hand and then at the woman disappearing inside her home. She definitely wanted to talk to Pinky about Autumn. But that conversation would have to wait. She needed to get back to the station for the Junior Firefighter Game Day.

Chapter 11

"How can Myrtle be in the slammer?" Nellie Byrd, Myrtle's best friend, demanded as a miniature firefighter in turnout gear and helmet raced by dragging a hose.

"Why don't we talk over here," Colleen said, not wishing the tourists to overhear the conversation between her and Nellie about Myrtle being locked up.

The miniature firefighter was, in fact, a child participant in the station's first Junior Firefighter Game Day. The game day had been Jimmy's brainchild—a way of bringing visibility to the work they did and raising money for programs—and it was proving to be an instant success. Her men were busy selling station T-shirts, giving tours of the engines and ambulances, supervising a meet-and-greet with Sparky, and taking pictures with visitors. The kids loved meeting Sparky, but the most popular attraction was the obstacle course.

At the start of the course, a child donned turnout gear and a helmet. Then, on the signal of one of the firefighters, the child hit a wood board with a mallet across a line, crawled through a nylon mesh tunnel, ran around a series of red plastic fire hydrants, carried a hose to three foam flame cutouts on sticks, picked up a squirt gun and fired at each flame, and then climbed a step ladder to rescue a stuffed cat from a child's basketball hoop that had been decorated like a tree. Each child finished to cheers from onlookers and received a special badge for his or her "heroic" work.

"Myrtle's being framed," Nellie said, marching around the perimeter of the fair to the other side where Aaron and Bobby were grilling food. "Ask Little Bobby if you don't believe me."

Colleen appreciated Nellie's concern. Not only was the woman Myrtle's best friend, but she was also a patrol specialist with the Lighthouse Wild Horse Preservation Society and understood how vital it was to the horses to have Myrtle on the job.

Bobby hung his head, having overheard Nellie's last sentence. It must be hard having Myrtle for a mother, she thought. Bobby couldn't escape her shenanigans . . . not even at the firehouse. She was reluctant to bring him into this conversation but thought he might have insight into who might want to "frame" his mother.

"You got a second, Bobby?" she asked.

Bobby set down his cooking utensils. "What is it, Chief?"

"Your mother's been arrested," Nellie said.

Aaron looked up from the grill, surprised.

"Brought in for questioning," Colleen corrected, in an attempt to prevent inaccurate rumors from spreading, and motioned for Bobby and Nellie to join her a slight distance away from the crowd.

Bobby exhaled deeply. "What has she done this time?"

"Witnesses saw her arguing with Denny at Pinky's house before the fire," Colleen said, her voice low.

"She's being set up," Nellie said.

Bobby shook his head.

"Has your mother been having problems with anyone recently?" Colleen asked.

"You mean more than the usual?"

Myrtle had rubbed a lot of people—locals and visitors—the wrong way over the years. "Yes, more than usual."

"Honestly, I try not to pay too much attention," he said. "It's easier that way."

"Didn't she tell you about how that ogre Denny Custis tried to coerce money from us at the society?" Nellie asked.

"No," he said, concerned.

"What's this about extortion?" Colleen asked.

Nellie stole a glance at the kids nearby taking pictures with Sparky and lowered her voice. "It started about six months ago. Denny tried to claim some of the public land in Carova as his; said that if we wanted to drive on that land we'd have to pay up."

"Like Mother would do that," Bobby said, and folded his arms across his chest.

"And if you didn't pay? What then?" Colleen asked.

"I guess nothing, since we didn't give him a dime. But I heard that one of the tour companies did and was pretty bitter about it."

"Why would anyone pay to use public land?" Bobby asked.

It was a good question, since there apparently weren't any consequences for not doing so.

"Rumor had it the company was allowing visitors to get closer than fifty feet to the horses to take pictures. I think Denny threatened to report them."

"That's blackmail," Bobby said.

"Like Denny cared about the horses," Colleen said.

"Exactly," Nellie said.

"But what does this have to do with someone framing Myrtle for the fire or Denny's death?" Colleen asked. "Myrtle wasn't the one extorting or blackmailing people."

"Don't you see? With Myrtle out of the picture, there's nobody on Tour-zilla's case about the horses. Everyone knows how Myrtle felt about Denny Custis. She's the perfect scapegoat."

"She wasn't still spying on Denny, was she?" Bobby asked.

She and Nellie exchanged a knowing look.

"Nell, tell me she wasn't still dressing up in that stupid disguise."

Nellie smiled weakly and shrugged.

"I told her to cut that out," he said, exasperated. "Maybe Mother should be in a cell. At least that way she can't get into any more trouble."

"Bobby Crepe!" Nellie said, scolding him.

"It's true," he said, not giving ground. "Father always knew how to keep her in line, but since he's been gone . . ."

Nellie gently squeezed his arm. "Your father had a special way with her."

Colleen shifted her weight. Children squealing, Sparky barking happily, and cheers from proud parents filled the air. Bobby clearly didn't have more to offer. "Why don't you get back on the grill," she said. "I'm sure Aaron could use the help."

Bobby returned to the grill and Aaron patted him on the back.

"I don't blame Little Bobby for being upset," Nellie said. "Sometimes Myrtle can be, well . . ."

"Myrtle?" Colleen offered.

Nellie smirked. They watched Jacob, the boy she had spoken with earlier about seeing Myrtle, running through the obstacle course. He wore a serious look of determination as he tackled each element at lightning speed and rescued the stuffed cat. Jacob's parents cheered loudly and Chip, who was standing at the finish, gave the boy a high five.

Chip caught Colleen's eye. "A future firefighter," he said with a grin and held the boy's hand in the air.

"Sign him up," she said and then turned to Nellie. "I'm glad you told me about the tour company, but it's a bit of a stretch to think that somehow they set Myrtle up. They didn't make her go to the house to confront Denny. She did that all on her own."

"Does that mean you're not going to investigate?"

"I just don't see the connection. I wish I could do more." Colleen moved to go.

"Wait," Nellie said, grabbing her arm. "What if someone knew Myrtle was at the house, waited until she left, and then started that fire?"

Nellie's determination to clear her friend was admirable. But that's not what made Colleen reconsider helping her. Nellie's suggestion of another person at the house was a theory she, too, had entertained. Now Nellie was providing her with a possible suspect and motive.

"Okay," she said. "I'll let Bill know. While I'm at it, is there anyone else I should mention that you think might have an interest in Myrtle taking the blame for Denny's death?"

"The only other person I can think of who'd like to see Myrtle take the fall would be Rosalinda."

"Rosalinda Hawthorne? At the wildlife education center? What beef does she have with Myrtle?"

"Two words . . . piping plover."

"But Myrtle told me they had made nice and even successfully collaborated to get the tour vehicle sizes restricted in the sanctuary."

"A temporary cease fire," Nellie said. "Those two are too much alike to get along. Good for the horses and plovers, bad for peace and harmony."

"So with Myrtle locked up for the fire and Denny's death, both the tour company and the piping plover folks have their biggest headache out of the way," Colleen said, thinking aloud.

"Bingo."

She sighed. "Sounds like someone needs to talk to Rosalinda."

"You're a good kid. Myrtle always said you were her favorite pupil."

Colleen raised a brow, skeptical. "Myrtle picks at me because she likes me?"

"If she didn't," Nellie said, "she wouldn't waste her breath."

Aaron rang a bell signaling that the food was ready.

"Hey, Chief," Bobby called. "If you want something to eat you should grab it quick."

"Thank you," Nellie said, grabbing Colleen's hand and squeezing it. "You go eat. I know my way to the front." And with that she disappeared around the corner of the building.

She needed to tell Bill about what she had learned from Nellie and wanted to talk to Pinky about his relationship with Autumn, but right now her stomach was churning. Maybe there was a way to kill two birds with one stone. She crossed to Aaron and Bobby, who were occupied with serving barbecue chicken, hot dogs, and burgers to eager guests.

"I think I'll take you up on that offer," she said, reaching the chefs. "Can I get the food to go?"

"Sure thing," Aaron said, grabbing aluminum foil. "One of each?"

"How about two of each."

"Lady, you eat a lot," said a little boy behind her.

"It's not all for me. I'm taking some to a friend."

"A friend," Bobby said to Aaron, and gave him a knowing look.

"Is that food ready?" she asked.

Bobby tried unsuccessfully to hide his grin and assisted Aaron with wrapping the food. Since when had it become a big deal to take a friend food? Aaron handed her the food and two bottled waters in a plastic bag.

"Thank you," she said.

"I hope Bill likes it," Bobby said with a cheesy smile.

"You want extra clean-up duties, don't you?" she teased, and left to check on Sparky.

She found her canine pal resting in the shade. She could tell he was tired. Since the children were now occupied with eating and other activities, it was a good time to give Sparky a break.

"Come on, boy," she said, untying his leash. "Want to go for a ride?" Sparky pulled himself up, wagged his tail, and sniffed at the food. "Maybe Bill will have a treat for you."

She entered the station and nearly bumped into Jimmy on his way out.

"Hey, Chief," he said. "You leaving already?"

"I'm heading over to give Bill information that might help with the case."

"The homicide or arson?"

"Both, actually. I shouldn't be long." She moved to leave then turned back. "Oh, Jimmy . . . the game day . . . great idea."

Jimmy beamed. "It was, wasn't it," he said and exited.

She made her way through the building and crossed the lot to her SUV. She secured the food in a storage container to keep Sparky from sneaking into the bag, hopped in behind him, and steered onto Dolphin Street. She contemplated driving to the wildlife education center to follow up on what Nellie had told her about Rosalinda Hawthorne, then reconsidered. If Bill thought the lead was worth pursuing, he'd want to be present for any questioning.

Chapter 12

Colleen parked next to the Sheriff's Department, relieved to have left the frenzy of the game day behind and eager to discuss the latest news about the case with Bill. She hoped that she could convince him to let her talk to Pinky about Autumn. How she was going to do that, though, she had no idea.

She grabbed the food from the storage container on the back-seat, leaped out, and waited for Sparky to follow. Instead, he looked at her and yawned.

"You can't stay in the car, buddy. It's too hot."

Sparky responded by putting his head down.

"Treats," she said, knowing the word would get his attention. Sparky's ears perked up. He padded across the seats and jumped out.

She held the department's front door for the Border collie,

greeted the woman behind the reception window, and strode to Bill's office. His door was open a crack. She peeked in, observed Bill reading files at his desk, knocked, and entered.

"Hello," she said, Sparky trailing her.

"Hey," he said, his face brightening.

"I brought you lunch from the station," she said, holding up the bag. "Aaron, the guy that does the OBX Barbecue Stand, was on the grill."

"That sounds perfect," he said, coming around his desk and motioning to the conference table.

"I've also found some things out about the cases," she said, removing the food from the bag and setting it before two chairs at the table.

"Hold on," Bill said and grabbed a notepad from his desk.

"First food. I'm starving." Sparky whimpered at the food smells. "I'm afraid I'm not the only one," she added.

Bill opened a desk drawer and held out a bone-shaped treat for Sparky. The dog took the treat and flumped to the floor to crunch on it.

"Thank you," she said. "I had promised him."

She and Bill dug into the food. It was expertly cooked and seasoned with Aaron's secret mix of spices.

"This is amazing," he said between chews. "Now I see what everyone has been raving about."

"We should do well with donations today," she said. "So how have things been with Pinky and Myrtle?"

He took a swig of water before speaking. "They're in holding.

You should hear Myrtle telling Salvatore it's like *Orange Is the New Black*."

She chuckled at the reference to the edgy television show about female inmates. "Myrtle does have a flair for the dramatic."

"As long as she's not dramatic with the press. The last thing we need is someone thinking our accommodations are subpar."

"Please. Everyone knows what a tight ship you run. Someone could probably eat off of those floors." He looked at her, unconvinced. "Okay, maybe not eat off the floors, but you and I both know how comfortable the holding area here is compared to a lot of places."

"Maybe too comfortable where Salvatore is concerned. He seems completely indifferent to being released."

I bet I know why, she thought.

"What are you thinking?" he asked, noticing her silence.

She had been hoping to speak with Pinky alone to find out what his connection with Autumn was before getting Bill involved but didn't see how that was possible now. "It's just a hunch, but I think Pinky's protecting someone."

"Who?" he asked, picking up his pen.

She covered the pen with her hand. "Hear me out before you write anything down."

He set down the pen and leaned back in his chair. "I'm listening."

"You know how I was up in Carova with Myrtle before Rodney picked her up? Well, afterwards, I ran into someone who I think might in some way be involved with Pinky."

"By involved you mean . . ." He raised a brow.

"I don't know," she said. "But she's been at the house that burned and she knows Pinky. He could be protecting her because they're either in some type of relationship . . . or she had something to do with the arson."

"But why would a woman involved with Salvatore burn his house? Did they have a fight?"

She shook her head. "She wasn't angry with Pinky as far as I could tell."

"Then why would she destroy his property?"

"The target might have been Denny. I think she's part of the group protecting the piping plover. Apparently, Denny removed fencing from around the plover nests that were on his property. She had plenty of materials in her house that could have been used as accelerants."

"You were in her house? Who are we talking about?"

Colleen was hesitant to name Autumn. If the woman's only crime was being romantically involved with Pinky, then a lot of women would want to be charged with that offense. She'd hate to have their relationship exposed unnecessarily, since both obviously wanted to keep it a secret. Plus, Autumn was Fawn's aunt and that meant she was soon to be family for Chip. The last thing she wanted to do was bring unpleasantness into Chip's and Fawn's lives so close to their wedding—especially since she was supposed to be helping with the wedding, not ruining it.

"Couldn't I just talk to Pinky, see what he says?" she asked.

Bill's cheeks flushed pink. "What is it with you always wanting to give Salvatore a pass?"

"I don't think he did it."

He shook his head. "I can't do it."

You mean you won't, she thought. It had been worth a shot, but there was no getting around Bill. Continuing to try would only make him more suspicious about her feelings toward Pinky, as ridiculous as that seemed.

"The woman is Autumn Harkins, Fawn's aunt, and, I might strongly add, my guy Chip's soon-to-be aunt."

"Oh."

"Now you see why I want to handle this delicately. There could be repercussions at the station."

He nodded, fully appreciating the predicament she was in. "Tell me what you know."

She briefly ran down her meeting with Autumn, her observation of the accelerants, and Autumn's apparent concern over her ex as Bill scribbled notes and asked follow-up questions. When she was done, he put down the pen and cracked his knuckles. He didn't like it, but he agreed that it would be best for Colleen to talk to Pinky. She could speak with him in an interview room and Bill could listen and watch from behind the two-way mirror.

They left Sparky snoring peacefully under the table in Bill's office.

"How's it been in there?" Bill asked Rodney when they reached the door to the holding area.

"Quiet. At least the singing has stopped."

"Singing?" Colleen and Bill said in unison.

"'We Shall Overcome,' I believe. She even got Salvatore to join her for a verse."

"You're kidding," she said, finding it hard to imagine what a duet between Myrtle and Pinky might sound like.

"You sure you gotta go in there and stir them up?" Rodney asked.

"I'm afraid so," Bill said, and opened the door.

She and Bill entered the holding area, which looked more like a hospital waiting room with bars than it did a jail. The tiled walls and floor gleamed in the bright fluorescent lights and the metal benches were covered with blue vinyl pads for comfort. There were even partitions near the sinks and toilets for privacy.

Myrtle crossed to the bars. "I knew you'd come," she said to Colleen.

"Nellie was quite persuasive," Colleen said.

"So am I to assume that this visit isn't for me?" Pinky said, feigning disappointment.

"Actually, it is," Bill said. "We have a few questions we'd like to ask you."

"Don't say a word," Myrtle said to Pinky. "Remember, nobody likes a rat."

Pinky chuckled, said, "My lips are sealed," and gestured as if locking his lips and throwing away the key.

"You two have become chummy," Colleen said, looking back and forth at the "inmates."

"We have to stick together if we're gonna survive in here," Myrtle said.

"Quite right, Mrs. Crepe," Pinky said, and grinned at Colleen and Bill.

Never in her wildest dreams could Colleen have imagined this alliance.

"And don't try to entice us with food," Myrtle said. "We're staging a hunger strike."

"And what, exactly, are you protesting?" Bill asked, not the least bit amused.

"Police brutality."

"Really, Myrtle," Colleen admonished.

"You're just defending the sheriff because he's your boyfriend."

"All right, that's enough," Bill said. "Up on your feet Salvatore."

"Anything you have to ask me, you can do here," he said.

Colleen seriously doubted that Pinky wanted Myrtle knowing about his connection with Fawn's aunt. She moved to the bars of his holding area and lowered her voice. "I met a friend of yours. She's quite the talented artist."

Pinky's amused expression disappeared. "I suppose a little time out of this cage won't hurt."

Bill unlocked the gate, took Pinky by the arm, and led him toward the door.

"Don't let them break you," Myrtle called.

"Don't you worry," Pinky said, and then exited with Bill.

Colleen lingered. "Since when did you and Pinky become so friendly?"

Myrtle straightened her shoulders. "I gotta have someone to get me smokes."

"You don't smoke. And neither does Pinky." She noticed a poorly drawn heart on Myrtle's forearm. "Is that a tattoo?"

Myrtle wiped off the ballpoint pen ink. "Practice for when I go to the big house," she said. "Don't want anyone thinking I'm a new kid."

"Cut it out," Colleen said, now finally losing her patience. "This isn't an episode of *Prisoner: Cell Block H*. You need to take this seriously. You could go to jail—real jail—for arson . . . and murder."

The door to the holding area opened. "You coming?" Rodney asked.

"Think about what I said," she said to Myrtle, and left her to contemplate the seriousness of her situation.

She followed Rodney to the interrogation room where Bill was waiting.

"This isn't the first time we've done this," Bill said, referring to when she had spoken to a suspect in a case last summer. "Still, like before, I'll be right on the other side of the glass. If he gives you any trouble—"

"He won't," she interrupted. It was sweet of Bill to be so protective, but right now all she wanted to do was get in the room.

Bill entered the observation room.

"You good?" Rodney asked.

"I'm fine."

Rodney opened the door. "Chief McCabe wants to have a word with you. You gonna behave?"

Pinky nodded. She had expected a smart comeback or even a flirtatious comment. The door clicked closed behind her. She sat across the table from Pinky. They stared at one another a long moment. Now that she was in the room, she didn't know how to begin. She wanted to help him, but if he wasn't honest with her he could end up making things worse for himself. Best to start with a gentle approach.

"You must really care about her," she said.

Pinky shifted in his chair but said nothing. This was going to be harder than she had imagined.

"Once Agent Morgan finishes analyzing the evidence, he's going to know what started the fire. If he finds out it was her, it won't be good for either of you."

Pinky looked at her puzzled. "Who are you talking about?"

"Autumn."

"What does she have to do with the fire?"

"Why don't you tell me?"

"Honestly," he said, leaning forward, "I have no idea what you're talking about."

"No?" she said, now not certain if he was playing a game or whether he was truly ignorant. "You do know Autumn Harkins, don't you?"

"Of course. I've bought her work; even hired her to paint a mural in the . . . Wait. You don't think Autumn had anything to do with the fire, do you?"

"She had access to the house and has plenty of substances that could be used as an accelerant."

"True," he said. "But you're overlooking one important thing."

"What's that?"

"I commissioned her to paint a mural at that house. Why would she destroy it and lose the job?"

"Maybe she was angry with you," Colleen suggested, not really believing it to be the case but wanting to cover all bases.

"Ridiculous."

"Or maybe she was after Denny Custis."

Her last comment took a moment to sink in. "This is absurd,"

Pinky said, pushing back his chair. "That woman wouldn't hurt a fly. She's trying to save the plover, did you know that?"

"Yes. And I understand Denny removed fencing on his property that had been put up to protect them."

"You've got it all wrong."

She studied his face. She believed him . . . which left only one other theory. "How long have you been seeing her?"

Despite the tenseness of the situation, he managed a smile and said, "Since you've been off the market."

That was the Pinky she had come to know and like. She could feel Bill's eyes on her but she didn't care. She had managed to get Pinky talking to her like he used to—which meant he trusted her.

"Are you and Autumn serious?"

"Autumn's a free spirit. It's one of the things I like about her. But she's got an ex that won't let go. Until that gets resolved, I don't want to be pulled in."

"Admirable," she said. "But it sounds like you already are."

"Since when did you become an expert on relationships?"

"I'm hardly an expert."

He glanced at the two-way mirror and then back at Colleen. "I hope that sheriff knows what a lucky man he is."

"Okay," she said, not wanting to get into a conversation with Pinky about Bill.

"Love is crazy, isn't it?"

"You're not going to start singing, are you?" she teased.

"I only sing with Mrs. Crepe," he said with a twinkle in his eye.

There was a knock on the window. A moment later the door opened and Bill entered.

"Sheriff," Pinky said. "So nice of you to join our little party."

Pinky was back to his old self. She had to admit she was relieved. She would hate for him to lose his joie de vivre. It was part of his charm.

"Just so we're clear," Bill said, all business, "where were you Sunday morning when your house was on fire?"

"With Ms. Harkins," Pinky said. "We had an early breakfast. Once you tell her I told you, she'll confirm I'm telling the truth."

"What time was this?"

"Seven thirty."

"Why didn't you say that in the first place?" Bill asked.

Pinky held his head high. "Because a woman's honor was at stake. Whatever you can do to keep this information between us, I'd greatly appreciate it. She's been separated for two years but until the divorce goes through . . ."

"I understand."

She was surprised by Bill's magnanimity. Perhaps now that Bill knew that Pinky was involved with someone else he wouldn't be jealous of her friendship with the man.

"So am I free to go?" Pinky asked, rising.

"Once we confirm your alibi," Bill said. "Until then, it's back to the cell."

Bill motioned for Pinky to exit and led him down the hall to the holding area. She followed, relieved that she had helped clear Pinky.

"Thank you," Pinky said to her when they reached the door.

"You can thank me when we catch who set fire to your house," she said.

"Back to Mrs. Crepe. Who knows, maybe we'll sing a little 'Kumbaya' this time," he said as Bill ushered him into the holding room.

"One down, one to go," she said to Rodney.

"Yeah," replied the deputy. "But that still leaves an arsonist and a murderer out there."

Bill joined them in the hall. "Looks like we need to talk to Autumn Harkins."

"We could call her," Colleen suggested. "She gave me her cell."

"I'd prefer to speak to her in person."

She didn't want to tell Bill how to do his job, but it seemed like their time could be better spent tracking down the real arsonist and killer. She also wasn't thrilled with the idea of Bill being alone with the woman—especially after Autumn had disclosed to her how handsome she found Bill. Of course, she agreed Bill was a nice-looking man, but she wasn't sure she liked other women thinking so. "Maybe Rodney could verify Pinky's alibi while we pay a visit to the wildlife center and the tour company to rule out Myrtle."

"I don't mind, boss," Rodney said.

Bill was silent a moment. Colleen knew there were two parts of the proposal he didn't like—not questioning Autumn himself and her participation in questioning Rosalinda Hawthorne and the tour company owner.

"Okay," he said to Rodney. "See if Ms. Harkins verifies being with Salvatore Sunday morning." The deputy gave a quick nod. "And get a timeline. If Salvatore left her early enough, then there would still be time for her to get to Corolla to set the fire."

"Got it," Rodney said, and left.

"So where do you want to go first?" she asked, accompanying Bill to his office to retrieve Sparky.

"Let's start with the closest."

She thought about this a moment. Each had stakes in the game. Rosalinda's concerns were for the welfare of the endangered shore bird; the tour company owner's motivation was money. She would have started with the tour company, but it was Bill's case—at least the homicide was—and given how intense the summer traffic got on Route 12 it made sense to begin with the location closest to them.

She clicked Sparky's leash. "The wildlife center it is."

Chapter 13

"The piping plover derives its name from the mournful sound of its whistles," Rosalinda Hawthorne said while guiding a group around the Outer Banks Center for Wildlife Education. "They are on the endangered species list of many countries and their nests are easily disturbed, so if you happen upon one it is best to admire them from a distance with binoculars."

Colleen and Bill waited as Rosalinda finished her presentation to a handful of visitors opposite the central aquarium. Given Nellie's comment about Rosalinda being like Myrtle, Colleen had expected her to look the same, too, and had been surprised to discover that Rosalinda was a rather tall, thin-boned woman with thick, white hair tinged pink from too much hair rinse. From what Colleen had heard of Rosalinda's presentation, the rivals did share two things in common—a passion for protecting an endangered species and a blunt manner of expressing themselves.

She scanned the interior of the Outer Banks Center for Wildlife Education. It consisted of a beautiful five-thousand-square-foot facility that housed a number of exhibits about the natural and cultural history of coastal North Carolina, a centrally located eight-thousand-gallon aquarium containing native fish of Currituck Sound, a waterfowl decoy gallery, an auditorium, and a gift shop. It was also where Rosalinda spent her days educating visitors when she wasn't working with the Corolla Piping Plover Foundation.

"That concludes my presentation," Rosalinda said to the guests. "I now invite you to view our twenty-minute documentary, *Life by Water's Rhythms*, in our auditorium."

"She's finished," Bill said, watching the guests file into the theater.

Rosalinda spotted Bill and Colleen leaning against the railing. "May I help you?" she asked, making her way toward them.

"Ms. Hawthorne?" Bill asked.

"Rosalinda," she said. "Ms. Hawthorne sounds stuffy."

"Very well," he said. "Chief McCabe and I would like to ask you a few questions, if you don't mind."

"About what?"

A busload of visitors entered the front door and was greeted by another wildlife center employee.

"Your relationship with Myrtle Crepe," Colleen said, raising her voice to be heard over the din.

Rosalinda snorted. "I'd hardly say we have a relationship."

A child from the group leaned over the railing around the aquarium, teetered on the edge, and attempted to grab a reed that was rising from the water.

"Careful," Rosalinda said, rushing to his aid and helping him down. "If you want to see the reeds, we have a lovely trail out back."

The child smiled shyly and returned to his group. Apparently, Rosalinda didn't share Myrtle's gruff way with children.

"Perhaps we could speak away from the guests," Bill suggested.

"I can't give you much time. Whatever you've got to say, Sheriff, spit it out."

Bill's brows raised in surprise at her tone.

"I understand you and Myrtle visited the legislature together regarding the size of the tour company vehicles," Colleen said.

"Having a common enemy makes for strange allies. That doesn't mean I'm friends with the woman."

"How would you characterize your relationship, then?" Bill asked.

"Let's just say she has her way of seeing things and I have mine."

"Regarding the piping plover?" Colleen asked.

"Regarding a lot of things."

There was plainly no love lost between Myrtle and Rosalinda. Perhaps Nellie was right about Rosalinda wanting her nemesis out of the picture.

"Where were you Sunday morning?" Bill asked.

"At home watching *Sunrise Sunday* and chatting on the phone with my son and grandkids."

"I'm assuming you can verify that," he said, removing his notepad.

Rosalinda put a hand on her hip. "What's this really about?"

"We understand life might be easier for you and the piping plover foundation with Mrs. Crepe out of the picture," Bill said, getting straight to the point.

Rosalinda waved his comment off. "Crepe may be a pain in the arse, but she's hardly interfering with our mission. Have you been chatting with Autumn Harkins?"

"Why do you ask?" Colleen asked, surprised by the mention of Autumn.

"If I've had any trouble, it's been from that woman. Had to kick her out of the foundation," she said; she lowered her voice and added, "She's a bit of a radical."

Was it possible Fawn's aunt had gone too far? Could she have set the fire and murdered Denny for interfering with the protected shorebird after all? Maybe Pinky was protecting more than her honor. Colleen glanced at Bill.

"Radical how?" he asked, now laser focused on Rosalinda.

Rosalinda hesitated, then said, "She had some rather unconventional ideas about what to do to those who interfered with the plover and their nests."

"Such as?" Colleen asked.

"She wanted to tar and feather the cars of those who were in violation," Rosalinda said with a shake of the head. "And that's for starters. I couldn't have someone like that on staff. It wouldn't be good for the foundation or the piping plover."

Strange how Autumn had failed to mention her dismissal from the group, Colleen thought. "How did Autumn react to being kicked out?"

"She didn't. Given her antics, I had expected some type of big scene, but she simply said that she understood and left. That's the last time I spoke with her."

"When was this?" Bill asked.

Rosalinda counted silently on her fingers. "About three months ago."

From the way Autumn had reacted to the mention of Denny during her visit, Colleen thought the woman's dismissal from the foundation would have been recent. Perhaps Autumn's anger had been simmering on the back burner. She wondered what might have set the woman off—and Denny on fire—assuming that she was indeed their suspect.

"Anything else?" Rosalinda asked. "I'm in need of a bite to eat. Blood sugar, you know."

Rosalinda pursed her lips several times. Was the woman really in need of food or was she attempting to get rid of them?

"You were quick to bring up Autumn Harkins," Colleen said. "Why is that?"

Bill raised a brow, surprised by her question.

Rosalinda shrugged. "No reason."

"We're in the midst of arson and homicide investigations, Ms. Hawthorne," Bill said in a serious tone. "If you're withholding relevant information—"

"My only interest is in protecting the plover," Rosalinda said in a raised voice, interrupting him. The other wildlife center educator shot Rosalinda a look. She lowered her voice. "All I know is that if you're looking for someone comfortable with the idea of doing things outside the norm—which I think we can all agree arson and murder are—then Autumn Harkins is your person.

Now if there's nothing further, I really am in need of something to eat."

Bill paused, and then said, "I'm going to need your son's number."

Colleen's phone buzzed and her pager squealed. "Excuse me," she said, and hurried from the building leaving Bill to finish up with Rosalinda. She read the phone text as the pager's dispatcher simultaneously announced a vehicle fire in Carova.

Bill emerged from the wildlife education center a moment later. "Got the text about the fire," he said. "I'll meet you up there."

"You sure? It could just be another car overheating," she said, untying Sparky from a shady tree.

Despite the Carova Beach Fire Department's persistent education efforts, SUV and pickup fires weren't uncommon in the four-wheel-drive area, particularly in the summer. These fires were caused by first-time beach drivers failing to reduce air pressure in their tires, placing strain on the transmission and engine. The fires started when the transmission fluid overheated, gurgled over, and ignited.

"Go," Bill said. "I'll see you there."

She slipped into the SUV behind Sparky, slammed her door closed, started the engine, flipped her emergency lights on, and pulled away from the wildlife center. Their conference with the tour company would have to wait.

She made her way up Carova's beach highway as fast as the speed limit, crowded beach, and oak stumps would allow. Sparky sniffed at the air and squinted into the wind, enjoying the ride. She swerved around a particularly large stump, then picked up speed again. Normally she wouldn't drive to Carova for a call unless her station had been requested for backup; but given the recent burning of Pinky's property and the arsons on the mainland, it wouldn't hurt to check it out. It was only on occasions such as the April 2014 fire of the Duck Super Wings, a beach apparel and souvenir store, or the June 2013 fire of two Carova beach properties, that local stations usually called for assistance from their neighboring Fire Departments. The Carova Beach Fire Department was a good one and would certainly have the car fire under control.

Colleen found an access point—a sandy road that ran from the beach into the community—and tracked the smoke to the scene of the fire. As she had predicted, the Carova Beach firefighters were in full command of the situation. What she hadn't expected to see was a Tour-zilla horse tour truck packed with nearly a dozen tourists photographing and filming the entire incident on their phones and cameras.

"Take as many pictures as you like," announced the tour guide with delight.

She rolled down the windows, stepped from her SUV, and shook her head in disgust. The last thing she'd want while her men were fighting a fire was a bunch of people recording them as if it was a form of entertainment.

"Look over there," the tour guide said, pointing to a dune on the right away from the fire.

The tourists turned from the smoldering pickup to witness a stallion and his harem cresting a dune. The stallion bobbed his head, neighed loudly, and shook his mane, prompting "oh's" and "ah's" from the crowd and a bark from Sparky. One tourist jumped from the truck with his camera and scrambled up the dune toward the stallion. Colleen glared at the tour driver.

"Sir," the guide said over the loudspeaker, noticing Colleen frowning at him. "You need to come back."

The tourist climbed closer, took a picture, and then slid down the dune to the truck. He's lucky that stallion didn't charge him, she thought. While the horses were accustomed to sharing their land with people, they were still wild. On more than one occasion, she had witnessed a fight between the horses when one stallion had wandered into another stallion's territory. She could see why Myrtle had been having conflicts with this company. Bill arrived and parked behind her. Perhaps they could question the tour guide once the fire incident was over.

She squinted at the remains of the smoldering and hissing pickup. She had seen numerous vehicle fires. It appeared from the charring that the fire had started in the cab rather than the engine, which would be unusual for an overheated transmission. She searched for Carova's chief among the crowd and was surprised to spot Rodney. She caught his eye. Rodney shook hands with the firefighter he had been conversing with and strolled over.

"What's the story?" she asked as Bill joined them.

"I stumbled on it as I was driving through. Called it in as soon as I discovered it," Rodney said.

Bill cast an eye over the area. "Where's the driver?"

Rodney tipped back his hat. "I didn't see one."

The pickup was located off the road in an area hidden by brush. "Hunters maybe?" she asked.

"Could be," Rodney said.

Though not an unusual activity in the four-wheel-drive community, she had never become accustomed to seeing hunters with rifles creeping through the foliage stalking wild pigs and ducks and had always worried that someday a hunter would accidentally shoot a visitor, a reclusive year-round resident, a bird watcher, or horse. She was grateful that thus far that had never happened. She noted Bill's serious expression.

"What are you thinking?" she asked.

"Anything about that pickup seem familiar to you?"

She stared at the vehicle again. "You don't think . . . ."

He nodded.

"Think what?" Rodney asked.

"You said you called it in," she said to Rodney. "You didn't happen to get any photos on your phone did you? Maybe in the early stages of the fire?"

"As a matter of fact," he said, producing his phone. "I took a few after I called, once I was sure nobody was inside."

He held out his phone, shielded the screen from the sun so they could see, and scrolled through the pictures.

"That one," she said, motioning for him to go back.

Rodney scrolled back and enlarged the image.

"There," Bill said, and pointed to a logo on the pickup's door.

A portion of the logo had already been destroyed by the fire, but the letters "C.C.C." were visible.

"Custis Construction Company," Rodney said, and glanced at the pickup.

Only one person would set fire to Denny's missing vehicle . . . his killer. Whoever set the blaze, likely set Pinky's property on fire.

Colleen was convinced that someone had burned Pinky's house in order to cover up the crime of Denny's murder, and that the more they found out about Denny, the closer they would be to solving both crimes.

"Did you get a chance to talk to Ms. Harkins?" Bill asked his deputy.

"I was about to when I saw the pickup."

Given what Rosalinda had told them about Autumn's radical ways and the fact that the artist's residence was in close proximity to the pickup fire, Autumn was looking more and more like their primary suspect.

"I'm going to ask the Carova chief about impounding the pickup as evidence," Bill said. "Then it's time to pay Ms. Harkins a visit."

"You want me to go with you?" Colleen asked.

"I got it covered. I'll let you know how it goes when I see you at dinner."

She and Rodney watched him jog to the Carova chief, chat briefly, return to his pickup, and vanish down the sandy road.

"You worried about something?" Rodney asked.

She wasn't crazy about Bill being alone with the attractive artist. Not only was the woman a possible murderer, but she suspected the woman was a bit of a flirt. She had confidence in Bill's loyalty, but she didn't know Autumn well enough to know if she could be trusted. And something else was troubling her.

"Do you know Rosalinda Hawthorne?" she asked.

"Met her a few times while working events at Heritage Park. Why?"

"When Bill and I spoke with her she was quick to point a finger at Autumn as someone who might do drastic things in service to the piping plover cause. But Nellie felt strongly that it was Rosalinda who might want Myrtle out of the way and perhaps blamed for Denny's death."

"You think Rosalinda had something to do with Denny's death?"

"I don't know. Something's not adding up." Sparky whimpered through the open window to be let out. "Excuse me. I think duty calls."

She opened the door, but before she could leash the dog he took off running. "Sparky, heel," she called, knowing it was impossible for a Border collie to resist herding horses. Much to her surprise, however, he only glanced at the horses, then put his nose to the ground and weaved toward the burned-out pickup.

"Do me a favor," she said, calling over her shoulder to Rodney as she jogged after Sparky. "See if you can keep the tour from leaving. I'd like to ask the guide a couple questions."

Rodney walked toward the tour vehicle as she sprinted to grab Sparky.

One of the Carova firefighters intercepted Sparky and grabbed his lead. "Thanks," she said. "He doesn't usually disobey a command like that."

Sparky bore his nose into the sand and pawed to get closer to the truck.

"Looks like he's caught a scent," the firefighter said, then moved away to join his fellow firefighters as they waited for the tow truck.

The firefighter was right. It was the same digging she had seen him do at Pinky's house before she had spoken with Jacob. She'd wait for the forensics to come back before coming to a definitive conclusion, but Sparky's nose was never wrong and right now it was telling her that the same accelerant had been used at both scenes. This was the work of Denny's killer.

She led Sparky away and joined Rodney, who was gabbing with the Tour-zilla guide while visitors were busy photographing the beautiful wild horses.

"Hi," she said, joining them with Sparky and trying to appear casual.

"Hey, Chief," Rodney said. "This is Greg Snelling. His father and he own Tour-zilla."

"I've heard a lot about you," Greg said with a sly grin.

She resisted the urge to bop him. "All good, I'm sure," she said, faking a friendly tone. "How have things been going up here with the tours?"

"Business is great."

"Really? I heard Tour-zilla had been having some trouble."

Greg's smirk disappeared, and he stole a look back at the tourists to see if any had overheard her. "You musta heard wrong." He shifted his weight and rubbed his neck.

His nervousness was not lost on Rodney. "Rumor had it that Denny Custis was giving your family a hard time—trying to unfairly charge you for driving up here. That true?"

"Maybe you oughta speak to my dad," Greg said, climbing into his vehicle.

"How was it you ended up here?" she asked. "I haven't seen you-all on this route before."

"Like I said, you oughta speak to my dad," he said. "All right, folks, I hope you got some good shots of those beautiful wild horses 'cause we'll be heading back now. Everyone buckle up."

Colleen, Rodney, and Sparky backed away from the road as the Tour-zilla truck rumbled off, rubber tail flapping. There was clearly something going on with the Snellings and their company.

Chapter 14

Colleen bustled about the kitchen as Smokey and Sparky watched with curious fascination—cooking like she was doing now was not an activity they had witnessed . . . ever. It wasn't that she didn't know how to cook; it was that she didn't have the time. The closest she usually came was heating food in the microwave or throwing pasta into a pot and opening a jar of sauce. For tonight, she had considered a stew, pot roast, baked chicken, and a few other dishes but settled on what was probably her best . . . Swedish meatballs. The smell of meatballs simmering in a cream sauce, boiling egg noodles, and a fresh vinaigrette salad were almost too much for her furry friends to handle. Sparky perked his ears, waiting for a morsel to fall to the floor, while the often-aloof Smokey rubbed against Colleen's legs and purred loudly. With any luck, the food would have as positive an impact on Bill.

She checked the time. He was due in a few minutes. She had surprised him by inviting him over for dinner rather than meeting him out as they had planned. When he had asked, why the change, she had told him she felt like staying in after the day's activities, but truthfully, she wanted to remind him how much she appreciated that he was in her life—especially after his visit with Autumn. There was nothing like potential competition in love to motivate one to cook.

The television played in the living room. She was only half listening, using it more for background noise as she prepared the food. The bell tone signaling breaking news sounded. She cocked her ear and heard the WAVE news reporter announce that there had been another fire on the mainland. She reduced the heat for the noodles and dashed into the living room.

"We've received confirmation that there has been another fire in Currituck County, North Carolina," said the newscaster. "County fire and EMS are on the scene. We have reporters on their way and will bring you the latest as it becomes available. Now for the weather . . ."

She watched the weather forecasts and maps flash across the screen, but her thoughts were elsewhere. She wondered if Agent Morgan was on his way to the scene and realized she hadn't heard her pager go off alerting her to local emergencies. She surveyed the living room, remembered that she had left it in her bedroom when she had been getting dressed for dinner, and sprinted upstairs to retrieve the pager in case a call came in.

Sparky barked and growled below. Seconds later, the doorbell rang. She dashed down the stairs, checked her appearance in the hall bathroom mirror, crossed the foyer, took a deep breath, and opened the front door.

Bill gave her an appreciative once over. "You look nice."

"I clean up okay," she said, playing it off, and moved aside to let him in. What she didn't tell him is that she had spent a great deal of time agonizing about what to wear and how much makeup to apply—something she hadn't done since her college days. She had finally decided on jeans, a blue blouse that matched her eyes, and a little mascara, shadow, and lip gloss. Yes, she had thought to herself while getting ready, I must really like this man to be doing all this.

"Did you cook?" Bill said, gaping at the stove.

"Don't look so surprised," she said, and gently pushed him aside to stir the noodles.

"Well, I've never seen you . . . I didn't know you knew how."

"Sparky and Smokey are having the same reaction," she said with a grin, and gestured to the dog and cat, who had once again taken up their posts near the stove. "I hope you like it."

"It smells wonderful. What's the occasion?"

"It's hard to think on an empty stomach."

"True," he said. "But that still doesn't explain why the special meal."

"Wait to see if you think it's special once you've tasted it," she said, but knew he'd find it delicious. She didn't know how to prepare many dishes, but what she did know how to make was quite tasty—if she did say so herself.

She peeked at him out of the corner of her eye. He was admiring the table. She had set it with the nice china her mother had given her as a housewarming present—the china she never used because it was too nice for her everyday purposes—and had a bottle of white wine chilling in a bucket.

"Would you mind opening the wine?" she asked.

"Not at all," he said with such enthusiasm that Colleen wondered why she hadn't thought of cooking for him before. Evidently, like most men, the way to Bill's heart was through his stomach.

"Did you hear? There's been another fire on the mainland," she said, removing the noodles from the stove and draining them in the sink.

"Bet it's arson," he said as he uncorked the wine and poured two glasses.

"I've got a meeting with Morgan tomorrow. I can ask him then," she said, and set the food on the table. "Speaking of meetings, how'd it go with Autumn?" What she really wanted to ask was if the woman had flirted with him.

"Fine," Bill said, his cheeks flushing pink. "What?" he asked, noticing her studying him.

"You know," she said, serving the salad onto plates. "Autumn thinks you're quite handsome. I believe her words were 'He could give George Clooney a run for his money.'"

"Really?" A corner of his mouth rose in an impish grin.

"Try not to look so pleased," she said. She stabbed a radish and crunched it in her mouth.

He pretended to sift through his notepad. "Now where is her number?"

"Very funny."

Bill tried the salad. "The dressing is delicious," he said between bites.

"I'm glad you like it," she said, pleased.

He held up his wineglass for a toast. "To the chef."

She clinked her glass against his and took a sip. "Wait until you taste the rest," she said. "My family loves this meal."

"I gotta say. I never pictured you puttering around a kitchen."

"Get a good look. I don't do it often."

"I know," he joked.

She kicked him under the table and laughed. "Ready for the main course?"

"Bring it on," he said with delight.

She served the noodles and covered them with the meatballs and sauce. Steam rose from their dishes and Sparky's nose twitched. She spotted Smokey preparing to jump onto the table and held her hand in front of the cat's face to stop her. The Siamese rubbed a cheek against her hand in an attempt to charm food from Colleen. If there were any leftovers Sparky and Smokey would each get a little treat.

"This tastes even better than it smells," Bill said.

"It is good, isn't it?" Her dinner conquest was complete. "So, seriously, what happened with Autumn? Did she confirm being with Pinky the morning of the fire?"

"Salvatore was with her that morning but, given the timeline, I'm still not sure she or he didn't set that fire. There would have been time."

"But you did let Pinky go?"

"You've taken a particular interest in Salvatore's freedom," he said with a hint of irritation in his voice.

"Only because he obviously isn't guilty," she said. "You don't really think I'm interested in Pinky."

"Are you?"

The directness of his question surprised her. Was he really jealous? The notion was absurd. "Let's put it this way . . . I've never cooked a meal for Pinky," she said, and placed her hand on his.

His face softened. He squeezed her hand and suddenly it felt ten degrees warmer. "Thank you," he said softly, gazing into her eyes.

She blushed. It was still a delicate process, but they were ever so steadily transitioning from friends to . . . well, she didn't know what to call it. Partners seemed cold. Boyfriend or girlfriend seemed juvenile. Maybe what they had didn't need a name. Whatever it was, though, it was making her happy.

"Do you want another helping?" she asked, breaking the silence.

"Definitely."

She served him seconds before giving herself the same. "Do you think Autumn was telling the truth about being with Pinky? Maybe she's lying."

"I thought you were leaning toward her innocence."

"After what Rosalinda told us, I'm not so sure. Did you notice how close her house was to the car fire?"

"If living near the car fire makes someone a suspect, then I've got a lot more names to add to the list."

"You have to admit that it's an interesting coincidence. And

Sparky reacted the same way to the car fire as he did when we were at Pinky's house."

"Meaning?"

"Meaning I think the same accelerant was used. Meaning I think the same person who set fire to Pinky's house set fire to Denny's truck."

Bill was quiet a moment, considering what she had said. "You think someone murdered Custis, set the fire to cover it up, and then did the same with his truck?"

"Yes."

"And you really believe that person is Autumn Harkins?"

Did she believe Autumn capable of arson and murder? In her gut . . . no. But there were quite a few fingers pointing her way. The biggest one being Rosalinda's.

"Didn't you find it strange how quickly Rosalinda named Autumn?" she asked.

"Now you think Rosalinda's our killer?"

She sighed. "I don't know anymore. Everyone we've met had a reason to want Denny dead. Is there a person in Corolla that didn't hate him?"

"We didn't," Bill said. She bit her lip. "What? Now I've got to add you to the suspects list, too?"

"No, but he did have a remarkable way of getting under my skin. Who knows what I'd have done if I had to be around him all the time or if he had tried to interfere with my job. Which reminds me, we need to speak to the Snellings at the Tour-zilla office tomorrow."

"Agreed. And I'm still waiting to hear from the ME about cause of death for Fuentes."

"Our guy under the walkway. I almost forgot about him." She got an idea. "Jimmy's friend Aaron worked for Denny. He must have known Fuentes. Maybe I can talk to him and see if he has any additional information to give us until we hear back."

"Wouldn't hurt," he said, and leaned back in his chair. "I'm stuffed."

Her phone rang in the living room.

"You going to get that?" he asked when she didn't move.

"Probably a solicitation. They always call during dinner. The machine will get it."

After the fourth ring, the landline phone picked up with Colleen's voice mail message and then a beep.

A recorded message said, "This is a collect call from . . ." and then they heard Myrtle say, "Myrtle Crepe." The message continued with "at the Currituck Sheriff's Department."

"For crying out loud," Bill said, throwing his napkin down.

"She's still locked up?" she asked with surprise, and hurried to the living room as the message continued with: "To accept the call, press one. To refuse the call, press two. To block all future calls—"

Colleen hit the button to accept the call and put Myrtle on speaker. "Myrtle," she said, eyeing Bill as he joined her in the living room, "why are you calling me?"

"I need to talk to Sheriff Dorman. I figured he was with you."

She signaled Bill to stay quiet. "Why would you think that?"

"He's your boyfriend, right?" came the reply.

Colleen avoided looking at Bill.

"So is he there or not?" Myrtle asked.

"I'm right here," Bill said, stepping forward.

"You cut Salvatore loose," she said. "So when am I getting out?"

"Why are you keeping her?" Colleen whispered.

"She admitted to tracking Custis to the scene and arguing with him. She has no alibi," he whispered back.

"Hey," Myrtle said. "My minutes are ticking away here. Am I getting out or what?"

"Come on, Bill," Colleen whispered. "Let her out."

He studied her a moment and then said toward the phone, "All right. Given your ties to the community I don't see you as a flight risk, but I'm releasing you under Chief McCabe's supervision."

"Fine by me," Myrtle said.

Colleen wished she had the ability to shoot laser beams from her eyes and burn Bill in the butt.

"As soon as I'm out I'll pack my bags and be right over," Myrtle said.

Colleen motioned to Bill as if to say "See?" and his amused smile disappeared.

"That's not necessary, Mrs. Crepe," Bill swiftly added. "Chief McCabe will just be responsible for you."

"How's she going to do that if I don't stay at her house?"

"I trust you," Colleen said. "I know you wouldn't do anything to put me or my job in jeopardy, isn't that right?" There was silence on the other end. "Myrtle?"

"Right, right," Myrtle said. "Now can you call your deputy?"

"I'm on it," Bill said and hit the button to disconnect.

Colleen stared at Bill in disbelief. It wasn't like her to be at a loss for words, but she couldn't imagine what she had done to deserve being saddled with Myrtle. "You didn't like the meal? Is that it?" she finally said.

"You believe she's innocent, right?" he asked.

"Of course."

"Even though she's still our primary suspect."

"Yes."

"That's why I released her."

"I don't understand," she said, puzzled.

He gently took her face in his hands. "I've learned to believe in that gut of yours, McCabe. That's why I cut her loose."

She gazed up at him. The way he was looking at her now, it made it hard to stay mad at him.

"And I could only hold her for twenty-four hours anyway," he added.

She took his hands in hers. "You still could have kept her there overnight."

"Have you seen those benches? They're fine for a few hours but Mrs. Crepe would be a pretzel by the morning if she slept on them."

She smiled. "You don't think she did it either."

"No," he said, and wrapped his arms around her waist.

"So why'd you make me Myrtle's overseer?"

"Because you're the only person I know that can keep her in line. And she respects you."

"Is that your version of sweet talk?" she joked.

He shrugged. "Maybe."

Smokey meowed loudly at their feet, and they discovered the cat and Sparky staring up at them expectantly.

"Looks like some critters would like leftovers," she said with a chuckle.

"I don't blame them," he said. "The dinner was delicious. Thank you."

He leaned down and kissed her sweetly on the lips. Her heart raced, competing with the sound of the clock ticking on the mantel. Yes, she thought, I could get used to this.

Chapter 15

"*What are you doing* here?" Colleen asked Myrtle, who was standing on her front porch, suitcase in hand.

"Reporting for supervision or duty or whatever it is you report for when under house arrest," she said, marching past Colleen into the house.

"You're not under arrest, house or otherwise," Colleen said, still holding the door open.

Myrtle scanned the living room, the kitchen, and then up the stairs. "Where's your boyfriend the sheriff?"

"He's not here," she said, curtly. "And stop calling him my boyfriend."

"That's what he is, isn't he?" Myrtle asked.

"I'm not going to discuss this with you. Now would you mind leaving . . . please? I've got a meeting with the arson investigator."

"Relax. It's only seven." Myrtle scooped Smokey from the floor. "Smokey, wouldn't you like it if Myrtle stayed for a little while?" she asked in a baby voice.

Smokey purred and blinked kisses at the woman. The cat had taken to Myrtle after she had spent some time staying with Colleen last summer. Traitor, Colleen thought, watching the two rub cheeks. It was no use. She was stuck with Myrtle, at least for a few minutes while she ate breakfast before heading to the mainland for a meeting with Agent Morgan.

"Can I get you anything? Coffee? Tea?" she asked, closing the door.

"Coffee would be great," Myrtle said, carrying Smokey into the living room and making herself at home on the sofa.

She padded into the kitchen to prepare Myrtle's coffee. The television clicked on.

"Did you see the report on the mainland arson?" Myrtle called from the other room. "Now that's a real sicko. I read some people get their jollies from setting things on fire. Bet this guy is like that."

"Myrtle!" she said, throwing her former schoolteacher a look of disapproval.

"What?"

Colleen was glad Bill wasn't still at her house and that she had had time to straighten up the place and get ready before Myrtle's unexpected arrival. She wasn't sure he would have liked the teasing about being her boyfriend or the talk of men getting their "jollies" by setting fires. She carried the mug of coffee to Myrtle and set it on the table in front of the sofa.

"You got anything to eat?" Myrtle asked. "Maybe a pastry or doughnut?"

"All I have is cereal or a breakfast bar. Take your pick."

"Breakfast bar," Myrtle said, and rubbed Smokey's belly.

She retrieved two breakfast bars from the kitchen, one for Myrtle and one for herself, returned to the living room, sat on the chair next to the sofa, and handed Myrtle a bar. "No disguise today, I see."

"No need for it."

"I don't think there was ever a need for it."

"Now you sound like Bobby."

"I'm serious. If you were trying to keep Denny from recognizing you, you needn't have bothered. From what I observed, the man was blind as a bat."

"You know bats aren't really blind. They can detect—"

"You're missing the point," she interrupted, not wanting to hear a science lecture on bats. "The man had terrible vision. He wouldn't have been able to tell who you were, disguise or not."

"Hmm, maybe that explains it," Myrtle said, thoughtful.

"Explains what?"

"He kept peeking back over his shoulder when I was at Mr. Salvatore's house. Maybe he was looking for his glasses."

"He wasn't supposed to be on Pinky's property, so maybe he was acting that way because he thought he had been caught trespassing. How'd you know Denny was there anyway?"

"It took me a little while of cruising around but then I saw his truck in front of the house. Nobody gives Myrtle Crepe the slip for long," she said with pride.

"From what I heard, he was thrilled to see you."

"Actually, he seemed a bit relieved when I told him I was there to fine him for coming too close to the horses. Didn't even refuse the paper. I thought for certain he'd put up a fuss."

Colleen's brows furrowed. "If he wasn't angry about that, then what were you two arguing about?"

"He kept yelling at me to leave. Said if I didn't my life might be in danger."

"He threatened you? Did you tell this to Bill?"

"Yep. Funny though, it came across more like a warning than a threat. Like he just wanted me out of there."

An idea came to her. What if Denny had been looking over his shoulder when Myrtle fined him because he wasn't alone? What if he was worried Myrtle might see that person and start to question why he was there? "Do you remember seeing anyone else at the house while you were there?"

Myrtle squinted—thinking—and then, after a brief pause, said, "No. But the whole time I was there I got the feeling we were being watched."

Colleen recalled Jacob's story about seeing Myrtle and Denny from the window. Myrtle must have an awfully powerful Spidey sense, she thought. Then again, she had been an elementary school teacher for over thirty years. Nothing like teaching grade school to give one instincts when it came to children.

While Myrtle's information was useful, Colleen had wanted more. "You sure there isn't anything else?" she asked. "Anything unusual? Did Denny have anything with him?"

Myrtle shrugged. "The only other thing that I noticed was cigarette smoke."

"Denny was smoking?" She remembered the matches found at the scene. Could Denny have used a cigarette to start the fire?

"Custis wasn't smoking, not that I saw. It was more like the smoke was blowing from elsewhere. Perhaps someone smoking on a deck."

"He could have left it burning when he went to talk to you."

"Maybe," Myrtle said, not convinced. "But he didn't smell like smoke. Not that I was sniffing the man or anything."

Colleen grinned at the mental picture of Myrtle sniffing Denny. She couldn't imagine that either party would have liked the experience. She glanced at the clock on the mantel. If she didn't leave soon, she'd be late for her meeting with Agent Morgan. He didn't seem like the type that tolerated tardiness.

She rose from the chair. "I'm afraid I have to go, which means you have to go."

"So I'm really not staying here?" Myrtle asked.

"No," she said, trying not to sound mean but wanting Myrtle to get her derrière off her sofa. "Sparky and I will walk out with you."

Myrtle hoisted herself from the sofa and stroked Smokey. "See ya' later, sweetie," she said and set the cat down.

Colleen collected her keys, wallet, and phone, grabbed Sparky's leash, and closed the door behind them. "Sparky," she called, placing Myrtle's suitcase in her pickup. The Border collie crawled from under a bush and shook himself off.

"You may not be staying with me, but I want you to check in since I am responsible for you."

Myrtle climbed into the driver's seat. "I'll see what I can do," she said, and closed the door.

"And, please, stay out of trouble."

"Now you really do sound like Bobby," Myrtle said. She started the engine and disappeared down the road.

"Ready, boy?" Colleen said to Sparky once Myrtle was gone.

Sparky wagged his tail and into the front seat he went. Despite living in the area for many years, she had never visited the Digger's Dungeon, home of monster truck legend the Grave Digger. Meeting Agent Morgan there to discuss the arson case would undoubtedly prove memorable.

Chapter 16

The Digger's Dungeon was an odd spot for a meeting with a federal arson investigator but, then again, Agent Morgan was a bit odd. Colleen had texted him yesterday after the most recent arson to confirm their meeting. He had suggested getting together in Poplar Branch, since it wasn't far from the incident site and he would have completed the evidence collection and have more to share with her.

It was early in the day, so the traffic was light. She and Sparky quickly made their way down Route 12 with only a slight delay around the Duck shopping areas. Cruising the two-lane road gave her a chance to observe new construction, the latest in beach attire on vacationers walking along the path, and appreciate anew the Outer Banks and the place she called home.

She breezed over the causeway to the mainland and up US Highway 158. She had passed the Grave Digger tourist attraction many times but, not really knowing much about monster trucks despite Dennis Anderson's Outer Banks roots, had never stopped to investigate. Anderson had become famous in 1982 for building the monster truck known as Grave Digger in a Kill Devil Hills garage from old parts of discarded vehicles. When first competing with his piecemeal truck against more sophisticated trucks, legend had it that Anderson had declared, "I'll take this old junk and dig you a grave." He had since gone on to win four Monster Jam world championships and erected the current attraction and diner for Grave Digger enthusiasts to see versions of the truck up close, take photos, and purchase merchandise.

She spotted one of the retired monster trucks perched proudly atop a mound of dirt and slowed to make the left into the parking area. She parked in front of Digger's Diner and set off in search of Morgan.

Sparky pulled hard on his leash. She wasn't surprised, given all the wonderful dirt that lay ahead on a truck course. She scanned the grounds. A woman took pictures of a man and his two children in front of one of the trucks, which appeared to sit precariously on its nose. The kids and father smiled broadly. Anything that could make people that happy couldn't be all bad.

"You here to see the dungeon?" a man sporting a black baseball cap, black T-shirt, and cargo shorts asked.

"Actually, I'm meeting someone," she said.

"You must be Chief McCabe. Come with me."

She watched the man, stunned for a second that he knew who she was, then hurried after him toward a building that read Digger's Dungeon. She had never been a fan of scary movies or haunted houses, and under normal circumstances would have been wary of going into anything called a dungeon, but the man seemed to be expecting her, which could only mean that Agent Morgan had asked him to keep a lookout for her and that the investigator must be inside.

"The dog's welcome to come in if you'd like," the man said, and held open the door.

She entered and turned to thank him but he was already gone, busy helping new arrivals. She cast an eye over the interior and was surprised to discover a working garage with various incarnations of trucks being assembled at bays. She heard men's voices and traced them to what must be the latest version of the Grave Digger.

"Agent Morgan?" she called.

Morgan popped out from behind an enormous wheel. "There you are," he said, and checked his wristwatch. "Right on time." He peered under the truck. "Thanks for the tour, Eddie," he said, and then shifted his attention to Colleen. "And who is this?" he asked, rubbing Sparky on the head.

"Sparky," she said with pride.

"Border collie. Smart dogs. Love to work."

Her brows raised in surprise. "You have a Border collie?"

"When I was a boy," he said, wistful, and for a moment became lost in the memory of a beloved pet.

She waited, uncertain how long this moment would last. Sparky must have been uncertain, too, because he gave a short bark and snapped Morgan out of his reverie.

"You know much about the Grave Digger?" he asked, motioning to the enormous vehicle before her.

"Not really," she said, somewhat embarrassed to be admitting her ignorance, given where they were.

"A wonderful story of determination, ingenuity, and persistence."

"Are you talking about the truck?" she asked, wondering if Agent Morgan was even stranger than she had imagined.

"Don't be daft. I mean Dennis Anderson, Grave Digger's builder."

"Ah," she said with relief.

"People first judged his truck by its appearance. But appearances can be deceiving. Like your arsonist back in Corolla."

"That's why you brought me here," she said. "To help me draw comparisons to the case."

"No," he said, moving toward the door. "I'm a big fan. Have been since the eighties. I knew I'd be finished with the latest incident and figured I could grab a bite here before heading back to the lab. Always wanted to see this place."

Colleen followed him outside toward the diner. They took a detour around the back of the garage and she was surprised to find a mini-farm complete with goats, chickens, and two pigs in the back. Sparky tugged against his leash, eager to give chase. Morgan studied the animals a moment before continuing toward the eatery.

"You hungry, McCabe?"

"I guess I could eat."

She tied Sparky to a picnic bench under an umbrella where he could enjoy the goats and chickens from a safe distance. He sat, focused on their every move, and didn't even respond when she told him to be good.

"After you." Morgan ushered her inside and gestured for a table for two to the waitress behind the counter.

"Over there's fine," the waitress said, indicating a table by the window.

The diner was brightly colored with 1950s'-style vinyl counter stools and chairs, black and white checked linoleum flooring, televisions, and monster truck parts on the ceiling.

"Heard the food's pretty good here," Morgan said, and opened a menu.

Colleen perused the menu and decided on the Slap Wheelies—the diner's fun name for pancakes.

"What can I get you two?" the waitress asked, bringing them two cups of water with straws.

Morgan motioned for Colleen to start.

"The Slap Wheelies and coffee please."

"And you, sir?" the waitress asked.

"I'll try the Digger Dogs."

"Mustard, ketchup, onion, or relish?"

"All of it," he said, pleased. "And water will be fine."

"One Slap Wheelies with coffee and one Digger Dogs with the works coming right up." The waitress removed the menus and retreated behind the counter.

Morgan checked out the surroundings, grinned, then said, "So. What can I do for you?"

"I wanted to run some things by you regarding our arson case."

"Shoot."

She thought about how best to lay everything out. Morgan approached things scientifically, so it was probably good to stick to observations. "I went back to the house to see if there was anything I might have missed. Not that you missed anything," she quickly added.

"Go on," the man said, unoffended.

"When I was there, Sparky had an unusual reaction to the area, started pawing and digging around the scene. That in itself isn't noteworthy, except he did the same thing with the fire yesterday— our victim's pickup that had gone missing."

"And you're thinking . . ."

"That whoever burned the house used the same accelerant to burn the pickup."

"Seems likely. That it?"

"Could a cigarette have been used to start the fire? I mean, did you find any evidence of that?"

"Yes to the first question, no to the second. We do know your fella used an alcohol-based accelerant. Once we have the specific chemical makeup, we'll be able to identify the product down to the brand."

The waitress set down the pancakes and hot dogs and poured the coffee. Colleen eyed her pancakes. They did look good. Agent Morgan lifted one of the two hot dogs stuffed with fixings and took a big bite. A mixture of relish, mustard, and ketchup dripped from the bun onto the plate and covered the outer corners of his mouth.

"Eat," he said, chewing his hot dog.

She thought of mentioning the food on his face but figured there was no use since his next bite would do the same. She tried the fluffy pancakes. They melted in her mouth. I guess that breakfast bar wasn't enough, she thought.

Morgan took another bite, adding more condiments to his face, and said, "Continue."

She swallowed, sipped her coffee, and asked, "So what types of accelerants are alcohol based?"

"All sorts of things."

"Art supplies?" she asked, recalling the bottles in Autumn's house.

"Sure. Many lacquer thinners, paints, and varnishes are alcohol based."

Her heart sank a little. She had been hoping that Autumn was innocent. Now it looked more and more like she had committed the crime and that Pinky, by covering for her, was an accomplice.

"Look," Morgan said, finishing his first hot dog and taking a break before the second. "There are all types of products for all types of jobs, all of which could be used as accelerants. Take cooking, for example," he said, gesturing to the diner's kitchen. "There's propane, butane, and kerosene. Each of them does a job the chef needs but in a slightly different way. Chefs know that and how they affect the way the food cooks and tastes. Each will have their favorite. Arsonists are the same. They have an accelerant of choice. Like a fingerprint. Once we get the results back, we'll get your guy."

"Does the serial arsonist have an accelerant of choice?" she asked.

"Diesel. Fills the Molotov bottles with it."

"Does that tell you anything?"

"Could be he's a trucker or a mechanic or a gas station worker.

Diesel fuel's not uncommon in a Molotov cocktail but most folks use gasoline."

"Doesn't sound like teenagers up to mischief," she said, now understanding why Morgan had dismissed her theory of the arsonist being a group of teen vandals during their phone conference.

"No, but it wasn't a bad guess."

"And it definitely doesn't sound like my arsonist."

"He's most definitely a different shark," he said, and finished his second hot dog.

Now that he was done eating, Colleen thought it a good time to tell him about his face. "You've got some food on your . . ." She pointed to his mouth and chin.

He wiped his chin. "The wife gets on me about that all the time," he said with a chuckle.

She grinned.

He signaled the waitress to bring the check. Colleen pulled out her wallet. "No," he said, waving her money away. "You were a sport about meeting me here. It's on me."

She had learned that when a man insisted on paying, you let him. "Thank you," she said, and returned her wallet to her pocket.

The waitress came with the tab and Morgan handed her several bills. "Keep the change," he said, and pushed back his chair.

"Come again," the waitress said with an easy smile.

They exited the restaurant and she released Sparky from the picnic bench.

"Keep me posted if you have any more developments," Morgan said. "We should have those results back soon. Then you can see if it rings any bells."

They shook hands and went to their separate vehicles. While it had been a strange place to meet and a bit of an inconvenience, the trip had been worthwhile. Unfortunately, with what she had learned about the alcohol-based accelerant, it meant Bill was probably going to bring Autumn in and question Pinky again.

As she drove back to Corolla, she mulled over the information Agent Morgan had given her about accelerants and compared it to what she had learned about Pinky's house and Denny's vehicle fires. So far, what did she know? Sometime on Sunday morning Denny had driven to Pinky's house—for what reason she still wasn't sure—and gained access to the property. Myrtle tracked him to the house to confront him about interfering with the horses. He had seemed distracted and Myrtle noticed the smell of cigarettes. Jacob witnessed them arguing, Myrtle left, and then someone murdered Denny, started the fire with an alcohol-based accelerant, took his pickup, ditched it in an overgrown area of Carova, and came back later to burn it to perhaps destroy evidence. She tapped her finger on the steering wheel. Why did the murderer/arsonist return later to burn Denny's pickup instead of burning it right away? Had he been interrupted when he drove it to Carova or had something happened to prompt him to burn it? And if so, what?

She glanced at Sparky, his nose out the window. His reactions to the house and car had been the same. While he wasn't trained for detecting solvents like the canines working as part of special investigation units, he did have the ability to recognize similar smells and track a scent. He hadn't been with her when she had visited Autumn. She wondered how he might have acted had he had a chance to sniff out her property. Would it be possible to pay Autumn a visit under the guise of planning for Fawn and Chip's wedding and see?

She returned to the Outer Banks and slowed behind traffic on northbound Route 12. She and Bill had yet to meet with the Tourzilla owner. If anyone had a reason for murder, it was a business that stood to lose their solid reputation and hundreds of thousands of dollars if it was revealed they weren't abiding by the law and were endangering the horses. Why had she been so quick to zero in on Autumn when she and Bill had yet to talk to all of those who had motive? She shouldn't jump to conclusions about Autumn, even if she was a strong suspect. And what about Rosalinda Hawthorne? How far would she take defending the piping plover? Was it possible she had fingered Autumn as a way of throwing them off her trail? She sighed. Had Denny made a foe of everyone in Corolla? She suspected the answer was probably in the affirmative. But even if that were the case and every citizen in Corolla and Carova had a reason for detesting him, not everyone would want to do him harm. And out of the group of people who would, only a select few would have the motivation and means to carry out the deed.

"I don't have a clue about this one," she said aloud, prompting Sparky to turn from the window and blink affectionately at her. She rubbed his ear. Even Sparky had a reason to dislike Denny after being teased with food. She came to a stop as the car ahead of her waited for a break in the oncoming traffic in order to make a left. A team of men unloading plywood from a truck at a construction site caught her attention and she thought of Denny's crew. Perhaps they could give her insight into their former boss. After all, she knew next to nothing about him other than what was publically known and that most people disliked him.

There was also another victim she knew little about . . . Michael Hector Fuentes. Who would kill the man and leave him under a walkway to rot? Police often focused on family members and friends as suspects because they were the people that knew the victims best and would have the strongest feelings toward them. But Fuentes' family was out of the country.

Both victims were connected through Denny's construction business. What if they were connected in other—off-the-books—ways? Could Fuentes have been killed to warn or punish Denny? If so, that would be pretty thuggish activity for the Outer Banks. Not even Denny would have stooped so low as to knock off an innocent person. Or would he? She needed to find out more about the victims, and the people most likely to know something about both men were members of Denny's crew. It was time to do a little digging into Custis Construction Company.

The traffic broke and the car in front of her turned into a neighborhood on the sound side of the island. She picked up speed. It was still relatively early. She wondered if she had time to meet Bill at the Tour-zilla office or if she should get to the station. Shoot . . . the station . . . she was supposed to meet Chip ten minutes ago. She grabbed her phone and hit speed dial for Chip's number.

"Hey, Chief," Chip said.

She could hear the worry in his voice and felt terrible that she had kept him waiting. "Sorry," she said. "I'm running a little late. I was meeting the arson investigator on the mainland."

"That's okay," he said rather unconvincingly. "You still going to help me with the ring?"

"Absolutely. Give me ten minutes."

"Okay," he said, his tone brightening.

She clicked the phone off. How could she have forgotten about going with Chip to pick out Fawn's ring? A therapist would probably tell her she had repressed it because of her own issues . . . and the therapist would probably be right. It wasn't that she was opposed to the institution of marriage—she was all for it—it just terrified the living daylights out of her. Her biggest concern was losing her own identity in the coupleness of it all. She had been single for so long that it had never occurred to her that one day she might marry . . . well, not until recently. Given her feelings, she wasn't sure she was the best person to help Chip with the task of picking out an engagement ring, but if he could dare to love with abandon, then she could set aside her own issues and dare to help him with a ring.

Chapter 17

"We're here, for better or worse," Colleen said as she parked in front of the jewelry store at the Seagate North Shopping Center in Kill Devil Hills.

"You okay?" Chip asked with concern.

Don't ruin his day because you're uncomfortable, she silently told herself; she put on a smile and replied, "Let's do this."

They exited and approached Gold-N-Gifts jewelry store. A poster of a beautiful sunset in the window of the shop next door caught her eye and she paused to read the quote below it by Maharishi Mahesh Yogi, the spiritual leader who had introduced the world to Transcendental Meditation in the 1950s.

"Chief," Chip said.

"What?"

"You ready to go in?" he asked, indicating the jewelry store.

"Of course," she said, not entirely sure she was.

There was something awkward about helping one of her guys pick out a ring for his fiancée. She had suggested that Chip ask Autumn, but he had said that he wanted to keep it a secret and knew Colleen wouldn't tell. After repeated requests, she had eventually agreed to accompany him. Even though she greatly admired the artistry displayed in the work of jewelry designers, she had never been much for earrings, necklaces, or rings. She didn't know if she'd be of much help, but if Chip could put his life on the line every day for the community of Corolla, then the least she could do was assist him in choosing a ring.

They entered Gold-N-Gifts, a sweet store that had a reputation for offering a comfortable beach ambience, friendly service, and fine jewelry at reasonable prices.

A woman behind a display counter looked away from the customer she was helping. "I'll be right with you," she said in a welcoming tone.

Chip wandered along the cases and perused the contents. Rings, bracelets, necklaces, pendants, and earrings sparkled brilliantly under the glass. Display cards indicated the collections and names of the designers. She trailed Chip and glanced into the cases at the works of Lori Bonn, Gabriel & Co., and Evan Lloyd.

"There's so much here," Chip said.

She studied the young firefighter's face. He was visibly overwhelmed. "Why not concentrate on the rings since that's what you came here for."

"Good idea," he said, and redoubled his efforts.

The saleswoman finished with the other customer and

approached. "Welcome to Gold-N-Gifts. Is this your first time at our store?" She smiled at Chip.

"Yeah," he said. "How can you tell?"

"We remember our customers," she said, and then turned to Colleen. "And you must be his—"

"Boss," Colleen blurted out, panicked that she might be mistaken for Chip's fiancée.

"I was going to say sister," the woman said, amused. "I think this is the first time we've had someone bring their boss."

Chip turned a deep pink. Even his ears blushed.

Colleen patted him on the back, realizing she did have a useful role to play. "Chip's one of my best firefighters," she said with pride. "Since I've never done this before either, I guess it's a first for all of us."

Chip's shoulders relaxed and he flashed her an expression of gratitude.

"Wonderful," the saleswoman said. "I take it you're in search of an engagement ring. Anything in particular?"

"Actually, Fawn and I are getting married this weekend. The ring is a surprise," Chip said.

"Does the young lady know this?" the saleswoman asked, her brows raised in wonder.

"She does indeed," Colleen said. "And at the risk of embarrassing Chip, she's very much in love with him."

"Chief," Chip said, reddening again.

"Fawn's a pretty name," the woman said. "Would you say she'd like more of a traditional style ring or something unique?"

"Unique," Chip and Colleen said in unison and chuckled.

"I think we have just the thing then," the woman said, and motioned for them to follow her down the display case. She opened the glass and removed a black velvet tray containing stunning quartz rings. "These are lovely."

Perfect, Colleen thought, impressed with how efficiently the woman had identified a suitable stone and style. Fawn would love the spiritual power associated with the quartz.

Chip studied the rings. "What do you think?" he asked Colleen.

"They're quite pretty," she said honestly.

"The ancient Japanese believed quartz formed from the breath of a white dragon," the saleswoman said.

"Fawn told me once that it enhances spirituality and wisdom," Chip added.

"And the rose quartz is said to be the stone of love," the saleswoman said. She raised a stunning ring with a rose quartz surrounded by diamond-accented dolphins on a pink sterling silver band and held it out to him.

Chip took the ring. "It is nice, but I think it may be a little out of my price range."

"We have a discount for emergency responders," the woman said.

"How much would it be with the discount?"

"Hold on." The woman grabbed a calculator, punched in numbers, and showed Chip the display.

Colleen wasn't certain if the store had a regular discount for firefighters or if the woman had offered the discount in the name of love, but she wanted to hug her all the same.

"Wow, that's much better," he said, brightening. "What do you think, Chief?"

"I think any woman would be proud to wear that ring."

"Would you?"

She blushed. It was a moment like this that she had dreaded when agreeing to the ring shopping. "I'm not really a ring gal," she said. "But, yes, I'd wear that ring—especially if it came from the person I wanted to spend the rest of my life with."

Chip extended the ring to her. "Would you mind putting it on? So I can see how it looks?"

"I don't think that's a good idea. Could be bad luck, right?" she asked the saleswoman, hoping the woman would save her.

"I don't see how. People come in all the time helping others. It's not an unusual request."

Didn't they see that there was something massively inappropriate about her trying on an engagement ring for her employee? Nice try, McCabe, a voice in her head said. You know this has nothing to do with being Chip's boss and everything to do with . . . She noticed Chip and the woman staring at her, expectantly. There was no way around it. She was going to have to try on the ring. Otherwise, she'd look like the enemy of love.

"It may not fit," she said, trying to buy time.

"It doesn't need to fit *you*," the woman said.

She took the ring.

"Left hand," Chip said, eager for her to put on the ring.

"I know what hand an engagement ring goes on." She hesitated and then slid the ring onto her finger. "There," she said, holding her hand out for him to examine.

He took her hand and held it so he could see it more clearly. She resisted the urge to jerk it away, closed her eyes, and tried to pretend she was somewhere else. No use. She opened her eyes. The ring was still there. What's the big deal, McCabe, she asked herself. It's just a ring. But it wasn't just a ring. It was what the ring represented—the willingness to take a chance on an unpredictable future, to give up control in order to make room for another, to take a risk and make one's heart vulnerable. Every day she was willing to put her life on the line, but she wasn't completely confident she was ready to do the same with her heart. It wasn't that she was without feeling as Jimmy had suggested, but the exact opposite. She wanted to be sure the person to whom she gave her heart would handle it with care.

After what felt like an eternity of Chip and the saleswoman examining the ring, he finally said, "I'll take it."

"Wonderful," the woman said.

She slid the ring from her finger, relieved that her role as hand model was over. She took a deep breath and smiled at Chip. "Fawn will love it."

"She will, won't she?"

"We're happy to size it for you, if you know what size she wears."

"Actually, I don't," Chip said. "But that's okay, right? We can come in next week?"

"Absolutely. I'll wrap it for you and be right back."

Colleen sighed with relief. Now she could go home.

Chip grinned. "You should have seen your face," he said once the woman was gone. "I think you were more nervous than I was."

She threw him a bewildered expression. "I wasn't nervous."

He chuckled. "Yeah, right."

"Yeah, well you should have seen yours." They shared a laugh.

"Marriage is a big step," he said thoughtfully.

"Yes, it is."

The two fell silent. She wondered if he was having second thoughts about marrying Fawn, then rapidly dismissed the notion. Never had she seen two people more in love. Funny how some people know right away and others take years to figure it out. She and Bill were definitely in the latter group. She supposed how long it took to get there wasn't important, it was the getting there that counted. There was no point in trying to rush or force Cupid's arrow. She had never seen that turn out well.

"Here we are," the saleswoman said, returning with a wrapped box. She placed it in a gift bag tied with gold ribbon.

Chip signed the receipt and she handed him a copy. "Congratulations. I look forward to meeting Fawn when you bring the ring in for sizing."

"Thanks," he said, holding the bag with the ring like the golden idol in *Raiders of the Lost Ark*.

"And I look forward to seeing you in here soon," the woman said to Colleen.

"Me?" she said, suddenly panicked, and noticed Chip snickering. "I don't think so."

"We'll see," the woman said happily, then moved to greet another customer who had entered the store.

"Not a word," Colleen cautioned the grinning Chip and hurried out the door.

She unlocked the SUV and they slid inside. She stole a look at Chip in the passenger seat. He smiled dopily, truly happy.

"Fawn will be so pleased," he said, holding the gift in his lap.

"You picked out a beautiful ring."

"Not about that," he said. "The owner of Gold-N-Gifts donates items to the Feline Hope Animal Shelter for their fundraising events. By buying Fawn's ring here, I'm helping save cats."

She thought about the small animal statues wearing halos of flowers lining Fawn and Chip's driveway. "She'll be thrilled."

"And so will Aunt Autumn."

She wondered how much Chip knew about Fawn's relative. He had called her "aunt," which meant it likely he felt friendly toward her. Would it be appropriate to grill him about Autumn? Colleen still considered her a suspect in Denny's death and the house and vehicle fires. She would need to handle this delicately. If she pushed too hard or came across as being negative toward Autumn it could not only create an uncomfortable ride back to the station but perhaps put a strain on their professional relationship.

"Autumn seems to be doing a nice job planning your ceremony," she said.

"I'm sure she is. I don't really know much. She wants it to be a surprise, but she did tell us about the love quotes everyone will be bringing for us."

The love quotes. She had almost forgotten about them. She made a mental note to research quotes on the Internet when she got home.

"Have you known Autumn long?" she asked, trying to appear as if making small talk.

"About as long as I've known Fawn. She's pretty cool, stands by her convictions. You know, she even got arrested once."

"Really?" Colleen's pulse quickened. So Autumn had a criminal past. She'd be sure to let Bill know if he hadn't discovered the fact already. "What was she arrested for?"

"Back in the nineties she was protesting the World Trade Organization in Seattle. She chained herself together with other protesters and they arrested her."

"Sounds like she's passionate about things she believes in."

"Oh, she is," he said as if that was an understatement.

"I understand her passion now is the piping plover."

"I wouldn't be surprised. She's an animal lover like Fawn. You know Fawn and I are thinking of getting a Border collie puppy, like your Sparky," he said, and that was the end of the conversation about Autumn.

She had expected to get more from Chip, but he, apparently, hadn't heard about Autumn's work with the Corolla Piping Plover Foundation or why she had been kicked out. She questioned now if what Rosalinda had told them was true. Had Autumn really been banished from the group? And if she had, was it for the reason that Rosalinda had given?

Chip spent the rest of the trip happily discussing Border collies, how the Baltimore Orioles were doing this season, and his preparation for a national firefighting fitness competition. She was grateful that he seemed to have forgotten about the saleswoman's comment to her about shopping for an engagement ring and that he hadn't broached the subject again. She hoped his memory lapse continued when they got to the station.

They pulled in front of the firehouse. It had been a long but productive trip. She had spent much of the day driving up and down Route 12. It would be good to get out and stretch her legs.

"Thanks, Chief," Chip said with sincerity after she parked.

"I didn't really do anything," she said, not wanting him to make a fuss about it.

But he wasn't having any of that. "I mean it. It was a stand-up thing you did. If you and Mr. Dorman need me to—"

"We don't," she said, cutting him off. "But thanks for the offer."

"Okay then," he said brightly, and hopped out. "See ya' inside."

He crossed the lot, the bag with the ring swinging in his hand. She was happy for him and glad that she had been able to help, but she prayed he didn't make a big deal of their trip to Gold-N-Gifts to the guys. She'd never hear the end of it.

Sparky hopped from his bed and wagged his tail upon seeing her enter the engine bay. He trotted toward her with his squeaky toy in his mouth. She kneeled and rubbed his ears with both hands. Sparky groaned with contentment, then flopped onto his side, put his paws into the air, and exposed his tummy. She smiled and gave him a belly rub. It was nice to be missed.

The rest of the afternoon was spent catching up on paperwork, reviewing donations with Jimmy from the game day, and playing phone tag with Bill. She even managed to squeeze in a ride around the neighborhood on the engine with the guys, which was a welcome break from the roller coaster of activity that had been occurring over the last few days and gave her confidence that things would soon return to normal. Bill had had to delay questioning the Tour-zilla company owner due to one call for a domestic disturbance and another for disturbing the peace. Worse come to worst, she thought, they could visit the tour company in the morning.

She leaned back in her desk chair. Sparky looked up at her sleepily, then put his head on his paws. They could both use a little rest from the hectic goings-on. Footsteps on the corrugated metal stairs to her office alerted them to a visitor. She prayed it was just one of the guys asking her what she'd like for dinner.

Seconds later, Pinky appeared and knocked on the open door. "I hope I'm not disturbing you," he said, lingering in the entrance.

"Not at all," she said, motioning for him to join her.

Sparky leapt up and sniffed at Pinky's feet before wagging his tail and following Pinky to a vinyl-cushioned chair on the opposite side of the desk.

"Sparky," she called, not wanting him to bother Pinky.

Sparky resumed his nap at her feet.

"You look tired," he said.

"So do you." She had never known him not to appear perfectly refreshed. Even when he had been in the holding area at the Sheriff's Department he had seemed rested.

"I wanted to apologize," he said.

"For what?"

"I'm afraid I took a rather cavalier attitude about being brought in the other day. Upon reflection, I realize that that may not have been wise, not to mention disrespectful."

She leaned forward, almost afraid to hear what Pinky's answer to her question might be. "Was Autumn really with you Sunday morning?"

He smiled sadly. "I thought we were past that . . . that we were friends."

She scrutinized his face, trying to size up whether his answer was a clever way of avoiding the question or whether he was being sincere. What does your gut tell you? "We are friends," she said, finally. "But you and I both know people do foolish things for love."

"True. But love founded on deception is an illusion, a dream . . . and at some point you wake up."

"You care for her."

"Do you care for Mr. Dorman?"

She blushed. Okay, she got the message. It wasn't any more her business how Pinky felt about Autumn than it was his business how she felt about Bill. So he was protecting Autumn . . . Colleen hoped it wasn't because the artist had committed any crime.

"Don't you want to know what we were doing?" he asked, a twinkle in his eye.

No! she wanted to shout. Then she noted his amused expression. He's teasing me. "Okay," she said, calling his bluff. "What were you two doing?" The instant she asked, she regretted it. The last thing she wanted to hear about was Pinky's love life.

"Posing," he said. "Or at least I was."

"Do I want to know?"

"For a commissioned statue she's doing. She says I have the eyes and lips of a young Andy García." He stared intently at Colleen and gave her his best Andy García stare.

She squinted at him. Of course. The unfinished statue at Autumn's house. No wonder it had looked familiar. "I guess I see the resemblance."

"García's not bad for a guy who isn't Italian," he said.

"Why didn't you tell Bill right away that was what you were doing?"

"I had made a promise not to."

"Can I ask you a question?" she said, leaning back in her chair.

"Isn't that what you've been doing?"

She smiled. Maybe Myrtle was right. Maybe she could be a little nosey. But when had that ever stopped her. "Do you know what happened with Autumn and the piping plover foundation?"

He rolled his eyes. "I'm afraid Autumn's passion got the best of her. It frightened Mrs. Hawthorne."

"She threatened to tar and feather vehicles."

"Autumn talks a good game, but she'd never do anything that might jeopardize those birds."

"Given her activist history, you can understand why Mrs. Hawthorne was concerned."

"That type of behavior is in the past. Haven't you ever done something because of passion and naïveté? I have."

She resisted the urge to ask him what. Maybe on another day under different circumstances. It felt good to be chatting with Pinky again, and oddly, despite the serious reasons for the conversation, she felt recent events had shifted their friendship to another level. If he believed in Autumn then shouldn't that count for something? She had, after all, liked the woman. And didn't most homes contain alcohol-based cleaning solutions, cooking fuels, and other products—even hers? Was she now going to question Myrtle about the paint they used for the Paint-A-Mustang events or the supplies Nellie used in her go-cart business? If mere possession of such substances was a sign someone was an arsonist, then every citizen of Corolla could be guilty. She recalled what Autumn had said about her estranged husband.

"What about Autumn's ex? Do you think he could have anything to do with it?"

"I don't see how," he said.

"She indicated that he was a jealous type. Maybe he found out about you spending time with her. Burned your property to send you a message."

"And killing Custis?"

"An accident," she said. "Or maybe he mistook him for you."

Pinky raised a brow. "Because Custis and I look so much alike."

"No," she said. "I didn't mean to imply—"

"That was a joke," he said, aware of his own attractiveness.

Good. Pinky was his old self again. "Do you know where Autumn's ex was on Sunday?"

"I believe in Virginia. I understand that's where he lives with his new girlfriend."

"If he's found someone new, why is he refusing to sign divorce papers?"

"Who knows," he said, and threw up his hands. "Personally, I've always found looking back keeps one from moving forward."

"Very philosophical of you."

He grinned. "I have my moments."

"One I never thought I'd see is you and Myrtle as cellmates," she said with a chuckle.

"I bet Mrs. Crepe gave men trouble in her youth."

"I don't know," she said, not sure she wanted to picture a young

Myrtle flirting with suitors. "But she certainly gave us trouble when we were in her class. I still can't believe you sang with her."

"She has a lovely voice," he said. "Although I think she believes I'm some type of mobster."

"And you didn't disabuse her."

He shrugged. "Why ruin the woman's fantasy?"

"Let's cross our fingers that she stays out of trouble now that she's my responsibility." She noticed his puzzled expression. "Bill released her to my supervision. Can you believe it?"

They shared a laugh. "I've missed our little meetings," he said with sincerity.

"Me, too. But, please, don't go burning anything to try and get my attention. We've had enough fires lately." It hadn't been too long ago that Pinky had used burning debris as a way of luring her to his construction trailer in order to flirt with her. "Tell me," she said. "Do you attend the Chamber of Commerce meetings?"

"Sometimes. Why?"

"Do you know the owner of the Tour-zilla horse tour company?"

"Snelling? A real weasel. Makes Denny Custis look like a Boy Scout."

"How do you mean?"

"Custis was no prize, but I understood what motivated him . . . money, power, greed." Pinky shook his head. "With Snelling, there's something else going on."

"Like what?"

"I have no idea. But there's a screw loose there. The son is bad but the father is worse. If you're thinking of snooping around Snelling, don't. I'm telling you, he's dangerous. Best to stay away and let the sheriff handle it."

For the second time that afternoon, she heard footsteps on the stairs.

"Let me handle what?" Bill asked, entering.

"Sheriff Dorman," Pinky said, rising. "We were just talking about you. Were your ears burning?"

"No," Bill said, not amused.

"I stopped by to apologize to Colleen, or rather Chief McCabe, for my lack of cooperation with the investigation earlier. Your office was next. I'm sure she can fill you in. Please, let me know if there is anything I can do to help." And with that, Pinky was gone.

Bill watched him go. "Why is it that every time I turn around Salvatore is prowling about?"

"I'd hardly call paying a visit to the station prowling."

"And you don't seem to mind."

"He amuses me."

"You know he's still a suspect."

Sparky wagged his tail and leaned affectionately against Bill.

"Sparky's glad to see you," she said, eager to change the subject.

"And you?"

She came around the desk and took his hand. "We're *both* glad to see you."

He softened and looked at their hands. "I'm sorry. I don't mean to be jealous. We haven't been down this road before. I'm still figuring it out."

"So am I," she said, softly.

How like Bill to take the high road, she thought. In this moment, he appeared vulnerable and unsure, something she hadn't seen before, and she admired his courage in laying it all bare. She stretched up to kiss him when . . .

"Whoa," Jimmy said from the doorway. She and Bill broke apart. "I can come back later," her captain said, retreating.

"What is it, Jimmy?" she asked, collecting herself.

"Only a work order that needs your signature. It can wait," he said, rushing down the stairs.

"I guess we're not the only one this is new to," she said.

Bill grinned. "I guess not." He squatted to rub Sparky on the belly. "So, what was it Salvatore was telling you to let me handle?"

"The Tour-zilla folks. He thinks they're dangerous."

He looked up with surprise. "Dangerous how?"

"Pinky didn't get into specifics, but given what Myrtle said about Denny blackmailing them, it makes me wonder if they didn't have the most to gain with Denny out of the picture. You want to head over there?"

He nodded. "But let me take the lead. If what Salvatore says is true, I don't want you in jeopardy."

She resisted the urge to tell him that she could take care of herself. When two people you respect warn you to be careful, it's wise to listen.

Chapter 18

Colleen's heart raced as she trailed Bill in her SUV to the Tour-zilla office. There was something about Pinky's warning about Snelling and his son that had put her on edge. Could it be that they were finally zeroing in on Denny's killer and the arsonist?

They slowed and veered into the shopping area where the tour company picked up and dropped off visitors. Sparky wagged his tail at a dog jogging along the road with its owner. Normally, she would have left him at the station for such a trip, but since he seemed to have a scent for the accelerant used in the recent fires, she thought he might be of help. She was relieved Bill was taking the lead on their visit; it would give her a chance to snoop with Sparky.

"Here we go," Bill said over her cell phone.

It wasn't difficult locating the company's office. An enormous Godzilla statue stood out front dwarfing the large tour trucks next to it. People waited in the sun on benches for the next departure to the horse sanctuary.

Bill's pickup passed Greg, the tour guide driver, painting the signature lizard-type scales on the side of one of the large Tour-zilla trucks. Greg watched Bill pass and then turned and spotted Colleen. He locked eyes with her, a cigarette dangling from the corner of his mouth. She pressed on the brake and slowed to a stop. Her heart skipped a beat. The paintbrush and can in his hands . . . the cigarette dangling from his mouth . . . both were elements consistent with what she had learned thus far about the burning of Pinky's house. Greg glared at her through the windshield a moment and then, suddenly, dropped the paintbrush and can, tossed the cigarette, and bolted.

"He's running," she said to Bill over the phone.

"I see him," he said.

Bill made a U-turn and zoomed after the man. She yanked her steering wheel hard to the right. Greg sprinted to a car, hopped in, and sped toward the strip mall exit. She hit the gas in a race to cut him off and glanced out the passenger window. The man drove in a parallel lane of the lot with Bill behind him, lights flashing and siren on. The entrance was only fifty yards away. She clicked on her lights and siren to warn people from entering. Her heart pounded as she approached the exit . . . forty, thirty, twenty yards away. She held an arm across Sparky's chest, swung her vehicle in a wide curve to the right, screeched to a halt, and blocked the way out.

Greg maneuvered the car back toward the Tour-zilla office and skidded to a stop, obstructed by Bill's SUV. She anxiously watched Bill exit, weapon drawn, and inch toward the car.

"Out of the car," Bill said.

She held her breath, praying that the man didn't have a gun, and—in that instant—comprehended how deep her feelings for Bill ran. Tense seconds passed. Even Sparky appeared to sense the gravity of the moment and viewed the unfolding action with laser attention. After what seemed like an eternity, the driver's-side door flew open.

"Hands in the air," Bill yelled, positioned to fire if necessary.

Greg stepped from the car, hands above his head, and placed them on the top of the car. This isn't the first time he's done this, she thought. Bill cautiously approached the car, holstered his weapon, and handcuffed the man. She exhaled, cut her lights and siren, and drove to them.

"You always run when you see police?" Bill asked Greg, who was leaning against the car, hands cuffed behind his back.

She parked and exited with Sparky.

"Nah," Greg said as Bill removed the man's wallet from his back pocket.

The man eyed Colleen and Sparky apprehensively.

Bill studied the license and then placed it back in the wallet and returned the wallet to the man's pocket. "Why were you running, Mr. Snelling?"

"I know the drill."

"What drill is that?"

"Find the guy who has had a couple of bad breaks and pin something on him. You're all the same."

"By bad breaks, you mean arrests," Bill said.

The muscles in Greg's jaw tightened.

"Any of those arrests for arson?" Colleen asked, coming forward with Sparky.

"You're not pinning no fire on me."

"We'll see about that," Bill said, taking him by the arm.

"Man, I tell you I didn't do nothing," Snelling said, tugging against Bill's grip.

"Then you don't have anything to worry about," Bill said, and opened the back door to his pickup.

A black Lincoln Navigator flew from the direction of the tour office and came to a sudden halt. Seconds later, a man emerged and stomped toward them.

"What the hell is going on?" he demanded. "Greg, don't you say nothing," he added, directing the comment to the young Snelling in Bill's backseat.

"Mr. Snelling, is this your son?" Bill asked, stepping forward to intercept the man.

"You know it is," the older Snelling snapped. "What the hell is he doing in there?"

"He fled," Bill said. "Know why?"

"Since when is that a crime?"

Bill folded his arms. "In my experience, innocent people don't run from the police."

The two men squared off. The Tour-zilla owner was not accustomed to being challenged. It was taking every fiber of his being not to punch Bill. Snelling was not what she had anticipated based on Pinky's warning. She had expected a man hardened from a life of crime, someone you wouldn't want to run into in a dark alley. But the older Snelling was a short, wiry man with a slick of graying hair combed to the side in an unsuccessful attempt to disguise a balding spot . . . hardly an imposing figure. And yet, she understood why Pinky had warned her. It was the menacing look in his eyes.

"Exactly what do you think he did?" Snelling asked.

"Actually, we were coming to talk to *you*," Bill said.

That caught the older Snelling off guard and for a second Colleen saw panic in his face. But it was only for a second. "What the hell do you need to see me about?"

"I understand Denny Custis had been blackmailing you."

Snelling faked a laugh. "Exactly what could that man blackmail me with?"

"You're saying Custis didn't threaten to expose your practice of allowing visitors to touch and take pictures with the horses on your tours?"

"Absolutely not."

Colleen peered at Greg. His father may have been dismissing the notion of being blackmailed, but Greg's expression indicated he knew exactly what Bill was talking about. She approached Bill's pickup.

"Do you know what the sheriff is talking about?" she asked the son.

"What's it to you?" he snapped back.

She felt her cheeks flush red but calmly answered, "I'm the fire chief and there's an arson investigation . . . one that involves Denny Custis's death."

"I didn't have anything to do with that."

"What's she saying to him?" the father asked, trying to see past Bill.

Bill looked at Colleen and—realizing what she had in mind—turned back to the father. "Doesn't sound like you respected Custis much," he said, trying to distract Snelling.

"Not many people did."

She leaned closer to Greg. "You won't mind if I have the arson investigator collect samples of your paint supplies, cigarettes, and matches."

"Knock yourself out."

"That's enough," the older Snelling said, brushing past Bill. "Don't say another word, Greg, until I get my lawyer on the phone."

"But—"

"I mean it," the father barked.

She glanced at Bill. They sensed there was something more going on.

Greg stared at his father, hesitated, and then said, "I did it. I burned that house. Snellings don't take nothing from nobody."

Snelling gaped at his son, stunned.

"I'm gonna have to take him in, Mr. Snelling," Bill said. "You might want to call that lawyer."

"I told you to keep your trap shut," Snelling roared at his son.

Sparky barked and Colleen drew him away, not wishing to add to the tension.

Bill placed his arm out to block the father. "Sir, step away from the vehicle." Snelling glared over Bill's shoulder at his son and held his ground. "I'm not going to ask again," Bill said.

"Idiot," Snelling hissed under his breath. He pivoted and marched to his Lincoln.

Greg watched his father drive away and then stared straight ahead.

Bill approached Colleen, motioned for them to move out of Greg's earshot. "How are you?" he asked keeping his voice low.

"Glad it's all over," she whispered.

"I have to take him to the station. I expect we'll be seeing Snelling's lawyer shortly."

"You want me to contact Agent Morgan and let him know? He'll probably want his team to collect evidence samples for the investigation."

He nodded. "I'll get Rodney over here to make sure Snelling doesn't dispose of anything."

She sighed. "Looks like Denny messed with the wrong family."

"I'll give you a call later."

Bill pulled away and she and Sparky got into her SUV. She drove toward the exit and caught sight of the Godzilla statue in her rearview mirror. She remembered the paint can, brush, and cigarette Greg had tossed to the ground. Maybe she could collect them before Snelling realized his son had dropped the items and had a chance to get rid of the evidence. She steered toward the tour company, reached the area where Greg had been painting, and stopped. She checked to see if anyone had noticed her arrival but, because of the size of the tour truck, she was hidden from view. She found a Ziploc bag in her storage chest, quietly exited, and scurried to where Greg had dropped the paint can, brush, and cigarette.

She scanned the ground, spotted the discarded cigarette, and carefully scooped it into the plastic bag. She didn't have the proper containers for collecting the can, brush, and another bottle but decided to take them anyway. Better to have her fingerprints on them than to not have the evidence at all. She grabbed the items, put them in the trunk, slammed it closed, and jumped.

"What the hell are you doing?" Snelling loomed beside her vehicle with a large plastic garbage bin at his side.

Adrenaline surged through her blood vessels. What could she say that would distract him from the fact that she had been lurking about his business collecting evidence against his son? She noted the plastic garbage can filled with cans of motor oil, paint, and what she suspected were other flammable materials.

"You wouldn't happen to be disposing of evidence, would you?" she asked, going on the offensive.

He curled his lip. "I'm cleaning up like I always do," he said, gazing at her SUV with suspicion.

"You were pretty harsh on your son," she said, trying to divert his attention.

"The kid's an imbecile."

Despite the fact that Greg had committed arson and murder, she couldn't help but feel sorry for him and wondered how he might have turned out with a more caring father.

"Things might go easier for Greg now that he's confessed."

Snelling snorted. "He couldn't let things play out. The genius had to take matters into his own hands," he said, more to himself than Colleen.

"I'm not sure I understand."

"And you won't," he said. "But that company was going to be mine."

"You mean Denny's company? I find that hard to believe." She knew her last remark could backfire and send him into a fit of anger or challenge his alpha maleness and get him to say something he hadn't intended.

"Custis was so stupid . . . didn't even realize what was happening," he said, his chest puffing slightly.

"What *was* happening?" she asked, amazed that Snelling was so free with this information.

He squinted at her. "Why the hell are you still here?"

That was it. Time to leave before things got dangerous. "I'm not." She walked to the driver's-side door, jumped in, and took off before he could come after her or block her way.

She zipped across the lot—the collected evidence safely tucked away in her trunk. Even if the senior Snelling cleaned his entire office and garage, she would have material for Agent Morgan to use as comparison samples.

It wasn't until she was back on Route 12 that her pulse returned to normal. Pinky had been right . . . the Snellings were dangerous. She exhaled. They had caught the man who had murdered Denny and set Pinky's house and Denny's vehicle on fire and, best of all, nobody else had been hurt. Time to tell Myrtle that she was off the hook.

She made the left onto Corolla Village Road and drove to the Lighthouse Wild Horse Preservation Society headquarters where Myrtle had her office. It would be good to be free of being responsible for her former teacher. It wasn't that it had been a big burden, but Myrtle did have a way of stirring up trouble.

She pulled in front of the building and Sparky wagged his tail. The spot was one of his favorites to visit, especially when the society had a rescued horse available for kids to ride and pet like they did today. Not only did the canine love the horses and the children that came to meet them, but he enjoyed chasing Inky, the black tomcat that frequented Old Corolla Village and hung out near the society's office. She leashed Sparky and spotted Myrtle and Nellie supervising the horse rides inside a fenced area. Sparky tugged hard, leading the way.

"Hello," Nellie said, warmly.

"Hi, Nellie," Colleen said.

"My PO," Myrtle said to Nellie in a hushed tone.

"I'm not your probation officer," Colleen said. Sparky whimpered at one of the horses walking near the fence. "No," she said, not wanting him to harass the horse.

"It's okay," Nellie said. "That's Creed. Nothing bothers him."

Creed had been removed from the herd as part of the preservation society's efforts to manage the population. The horse was saddle trained and known for being good with children. His calm demeanor made him an excellent ambassador. The volunteer guiding the horse paused before them and Colleen stroked Creed's forehead. The horse blinked in appreciation and then was off again with the volunteer and his rider.

"You checking up on me?" Myrtle asked her.

"Actually, I came to tell you you're off the hook. Bill's made an arrest."

"That's wonderful. Now I don't have to babysit you," Nellie kidded.

Myrtle frowned. "How do you know it's the right guy?"

"He confessed," Colleen said.

"To the murder of Denny's worker, too?"

"No," Colleen said. "At least not yet. Aren't you pleased? Now you can do whatever you'd like and nobody will be watching you."

"You mean now you won't have to think about me," Myrtle said, pouting.

Nellie rolled her eyes. "How can we *not* think about you?" she said, and winked at Colleen.

"Who did it?" Myrtle asked, reluctantly accepting her return to ordinary citizenry and the end of her stint as Corolla's Most Wanted.

"Greg Snelling."

"Didn't I tell you those Tour-zilla folks were criminals?" Myrtle said.

"From what I understand," Nellie said, "the son has had a hard life."

Myrtle gawked. "How can you say that, Nell? Those are the same folks we've been fighting with about the horses."

"I know. It's just that you hate to see a young person ruin his life."

"I'm not sure having the father he had helped much," Colleen said.

"Oh, please," Myrtle said. "Next you'll be telling me all the problems of the world could be solved with love."

"It couldn't hurt," Colleen said.

Myrtle wrinkled her nose. "You're only saying that because you're all gushy over the sheriff."

"Leave Colleen alone," Nellie said, swatting at Myrtle. Then to further Colleen's embarrassment . . . "I think it's sweet you two are together."

"Thank you," Colleen said. "You know, Myrtle, I think you have an admirer since being locked up."

"Don't be silly."

"It's true. Pinky told me you have a lovely singing voice."

A pleased smile crept over her face. "He did?"

"I guess he overlooked the fact that you've called him a gangster," Nellie said.

"I never said that," Myrtle protested. Noticing Colleen and Nellie's raised brows, she added, "Well, I didn't mean it."

"Because you never mean what you say," Nellie said with a chuckle.

Sparky barked at Creed as the volunteer led the horse in another loop. "I'll let you two get back to the horses," she said.

"We were going to grab a bite later. You're welcome to join us," Nellie offered.

"Thanks, but I'm heading home. It's been a long day. Congratulations on your freedom," she said to Myrtle.

"Hmpf," came Myrtle's reply.

She grinned. All they had to do was find out how Michael Fuentes ended up dead under the beach walkway and all would be back to normal.

Chapter 19

Colleen reclined on the sofa with Smokey sleeping on her chest and Sparky at her feet. She half watched the late news as she processed the events of the day. The only thing that could have made her completely at ease was if Bill were there.

He had called her after she had arrived home to make sure she had made it back okay and to briefly fill her in on what he had learned from Snelling at the station. True to his word, the father had arrived with a lawyer but, much to his father and the lawyer's chagrin, the son had put his confession in writing and refused to see them. Bill had had to threaten to arrest the senior Snelling, too, when he became abusive, and the lawyer had had to drag the father from the station.

She had relayed her encounter with Mr. Snelling. She knew Bill would be angry at her for going back and risking an altercation. She also knew his reaction came from a feeling of helplessness. It was how she had felt when Bill had approached Greg Snelling's car after the man had attempted to flee.

After her conversation with Bill, she had called Agent Morgan's office and left a message about the arrest and her fortuitous collection of potential evidence for testing. As it turned out, it was good that she had retrieved the paint and cigarette. By the time Rodney had arrived and secured the scene, the older Snelling had disposed of everything. She imagined there would be a press conference once lab results came back. She had forced herself to stay up to see if any word of the arrest made the evening news and to get Bill's call when he was done at the station.

Now that Snelling was under arrest, she felt crummy about having suspected Autumn. She should have known Pinky wouldn't cover for criminal behavior and jeopardize his business . . . even if it was for a woman. She was relieved that Autumn was no longer a suspect. She liked the woman and it would certainly make Fawn and Chip's wedding more enjoyable.

The wedding! She needed to find a quote. She searched for her phone and noticed it on the floor just out of reach. Smokey snored loudly and soft bursts of warm breath hit Colleen's chin. She shifted her position on the sofa and the cat let out a chirp before rotating her head upside-down and covering it with a paw. She peered over the cat at Sparky. His paws twitched, dreaming no doubt about chasing the horses or running on the beach. She inched the phone closer with her fingers and snatched it from the floor.

Before she could begin the quote search on her phone, the television sounded the tone for breaking news and an image of a reporter on location appeared on the screen. Behind the reporter stood Agent Morgan with his team members and several law enforcement officers. She grabbed the remote and increased the volume.

"Agent Morgan from the special investigation unit will be speaking any minute now on the arrest of the mainland arsonist," the reporter said.

Colleen gently lifted Smokey, placed her on the sofa, and sat up. The cat cried in protest, then turned in a circle, curled in a ball, and fell back to sleep.

"Good evening," Agent Morgan, said, squinting at the reporters. "Tonight we're announcing the arrest of Earl and Tiffany Odom in relation to a series of abandoned property fires in Currituck County. We received a tip which led to a warrant being served on their residence where we found substances identical to those materials used in the arsons. It is still an active investigation so at this time we won't share any more information other than to say that we don't believe that any other parties were involved. Thank you."

"Can you tell us why they did it?" one reporter asked.

"Again, I'm not going to comment further," Morgan said.

"Are they also responsible for the fire in Corolla this past Sunday?" another reporter asked.

Colleen leaned forward, wondering if Morgan had received her message, given how busy he must have been with the break in the case.

"The Corolla arson is not connected to these crimes but I understand they have a person in custody."

He did get the message, she thought, and sat back on the sofa.

Morgan retreated with his team and the brief conference was over. She clicked off the television. Two arson investigations and a homicide case were now closed. Now only the mystery of what had happened to Michael Fuentes remained. But that could wait until the morning. Right now she needed sleep. She took her phone in case Bill called, flipped off the lights, and schlepped upstairs to bed.

At one o'clock, her phone buzzed on her nightstand alerting her to an incoming text message. She read: HEADING HOME. GET SLEEP.—B She texted YOU, TOO and turned over to grab a few more hours of sleep. Unfortunately, despite the arrests for the arsons and Denny's homicide, sleep didn't come easy. Her brain kept replaying bits and pieces from the day's events, trying to organize the information into its proper mental compartments. One piece of information didn't fit and, as a result, played over and over in her mind.

What was it the senior Snelling had told her? Something about getting Denny's company. She flipped the pillow and shifted to her other side. She had heard that changing positions could break a mental loop. She tried her back and even her stomach but it was no use—her brain didn't have any place for the information to go. The more she tried to pull at it the worse it got—like an unraveling loose string on a sweater. She sat up and rubbed her face. Okay, she thought, think about it, make sense of it, and then you'll be able to sleep.

She concentrated on her conversation with the older Snelling. Her adrenaline had been so high that she wasn't sure she had heard everything correctly. He had been angry at his son for confessing. Nothing odd about that except for the complete lack of concern he showed toward his offspring. But Snelling had also been annoyed by the fact that Greg had done something that didn't fit with a plan . . . and that plan seemed to involve Denny's company. The father had said that Denny hadn't realized what was happening, but how could someone take over Denny's company without Denny knowing? She flumped onto her back in frustration. You're tired, she told herself. Get some sleep and maybe it will make sense in the morning. She closed her eyes and forced herself to picture a peaceful place on the beach. Every time a thought of Snelling or Denny's company or Greg's arrest crept into her consciousness, she imagined a shark leaping from the water and pulling the thought deep into the ocean. Slowly, the thoughts disappeared and she drifted back to sleep.

Sunlight streamed in through the window, Smokey pawed at her face, and Sparky's tail pounded against the side of the bed. She inhaled deeply, pleased that she had managed to sleep. She opened her eyes and Smokey meowed. She rubbed the cat's cheek with one hand and scratched Sparky behind the ear with the other. Despite the night of tossing and turning, she felt refreshed and ready to take on the day.

She checked the clock. It was late. No wonder Smokey and Sparky had come to fetch her. She threw her legs over the bed. No time for a run this morning. She quickly prepared breakfast for the three of them, let the dog out, got ready, and then departed with Sparky. She was eager to chat with Bill about his night and to see if there had been any new developments in the Fuentes case. Once they figured out the mystery of what had happened to Fuentes, she could concentrate on her life at the station and with Bill. She was even looking forward to Fawn and Chip's wedding.

She drove south on Ocean Trail, her hair whipping freely to help it dry. Sparky watched with curious interest as her hair billowed in the wind. She touched the screen on her cell phone and dialed Bill. He picked up after the second ring.

"Good morning," she said.

"Morning." His voice sounded tired but not stressed. "I would have called, but I was letting you sleep."

"Sounds like you're the one that needed more sleep," she said. "Did you get any?"

"A little. And you?"

"Same. Did you hear? Morgan caught the arsonists. Thought I'd call him this morning to see when he wanted to pick up the evidence. By the way, Snelling didn't happen to say anything to you about his dad buying Denny's business, did he?"

"No," Bill said. "But I heard from the ME about Fuentes. He confirmed the proximate cause of death is strangulation, immediate cause asphyxiation."

"Strangulation is rather personal. You think it's someone he knew?"

"No way of telling. But I thought I'd question Denny's crew, see what they might be able to tell me."

She had wanted to talk to Denny's men, too. Maybe they'd have some information about the business and whether or not Denny had been planning to sell it. "What time do you want to do that?" There was silence on the other end. "Bill? You still there?"

"Yeah."

The tone of his response told her that he hadn't anticipated having her accompany him to speak with Denny's men. He was doing it again . . . their pas de deux, as he called it. "I know you don't like it when I get involved in—"

"It's not that," he interrupted. "I don't know what type of people we're dealing with. After yesterday with Snelling . . ."

He didn't have to finish. She got it. He was worried about her safety. She wouldn't push it. He was the sheriff after all. "Okay," she said. "Let me know what you find out."

"Thank you," he said, reassured.

"I'm at the station," she said. "Talk to you later?"

"Later," Bill said and disconnected.

She pulled up to the firehouse. It would be nice to spend a day with the guys at the station. She parked and headed inside, Sparky trotting at her side. She entered the bay and was surprised to find it empty. Usually there was someone around playing Nerf basketball or cleaning equipment. She opened the door leading to the recreation room. Never could she have imagined the scene before her.

"'To keep your marriage brimming, with love in the wedding cup, whenever you're wrong, admit it; whenever you're right, shut up.'—Ogden Nash," read one of the guys from a paper, and the entire room erupted in laughter.

"Hey, Chief, you're just in time," said Jimmy, waving her over.

"I got one by some guy, Stuart Turner," Kenny said, standing with a notecard. He read, "'If you think women are the weaker sex, try pulling the blankets back to your side.'"

"You know that from experience?" one of the guys asked, and Kenny nodded.

She joined Jimmy near the sofa. "What's going on?"

"The guys are reading Chip their quotes for the wedding."

"Jimmy, you're up," Chip said.

Jimmy rose, removed a paper from his pocket, and cleared his throat. "'People are weird.'"

"That's our Chip."

"Very funny," Chip said.

"May I continue?" Jimmy asked. "'People are weird. When we find someone with weirdness that is compatible with ours, we team up and call it love.'"

"You saying we're weird?" Chip asked.

"If the shoe fits, Chipmunk," another guy joshed.

"That, my dear friends, was paraphrased from the great philosopher and author of *All I Really Need to Know I Learned in Kindergarten*, Robert Fulghum," Jimmy said, and the room erupted into laughter.

The men were having a good time. She could only imagine what the wedding would be like.

"Hey, Chief, what about you?" Bobby asked.

"I'm afraid I haven't found mine yet," Colleen said, and received a round of playful boos from the group.

"I've found one," Bobby said, meekly holding his in the air.

"Let's hear it, Big B," Chip said.

Bobby took his place before the crowd on the sofa. "This is a quote I found by Josh Billings, whose real name was Henry Wheeler Shaw. It's actually about marriage but you could substitute being a firefighter and it could still apply . . . at least I think so."

She and Jimmy grinned at one another. Bobby was evidently taking the task seriously.

"Get to the quote, Crepe," Kenny said.

"Right," Bobby said and straightened his posture. "Here goes . . . 'Marrying for love may be a little risky, but it is so honest that God can't help but smile on it.'"

Everyone fell silent. Bobby peered at the group, uncertain.

"That was lovely," she said.

Bobby returned the paper to his pocket. Chip held out his fist and bumped Bobby's. "Thanks for taking my big day seriously," Chip said. "Unlike some of these bozos."

The guys jeered and booed. Sparky barked at the noise, and the touching moment was over.

"You got a minute?" she asked Jimmy.

"Sure."

She left the men to teasing Chip and entered the kitchen for a cup of coffee, Jimmy and Sparky trailing her. She found a mug and poured herself half a cup.

"What's up?" Jimmy asked.

Sparky whined for a treat. She took one from the stash they had in a jar on the counter and the dog settled to the floor with his treasure.

"I presume you heard that Bill arrested Greg Snelling."

"It's all anyone is talking about," Jimmy said, and leaned against the counter. "That and Chip's wedding."

"Yes," she said with a grin. "Never thought I'd see you guys reading love quotes."

"Hey," he said pretending to take offense. "We have hearts. I noticed you still don't have one. Better get cracking on that. The wedding is Friday."

"You could give me one of yours."

"You want to cheat on such an important thing as Chip's wedding?" He shook his head. "Shame on you."

"Fine. I'll find a quote. So can we get back to why I wanted to speak with you?"

"Shoot."

"Did you ever hear anything about Denny selling his company?"

"Are you kidding? That company was Denny's baby. No way he'd let anyone take it."

"That's what I thought," she said. "You think it's possible someone could steal a company or maybe kill its owner to take it over?"

"You think Snelling killed Denny to get his company?"

"No . . . maybe . . . I don't know. Nothing's making sense."

He studied her. "What's bothering you?"

"Fuentes. We still don't know what exactly happened to him."

"You have a theory?"

"I'm afraid I don't. Maybe Fuentes had some enemies," she offered.

"Wouldn't Bill have uncovered that by now?"

"The guy's family is in Mexico and he had no known problems with anyone. So how does he end up like he did?"

He shrugged. "Could be he was in the wrong place at the wrong time. It happens."

She didn't think it likely Fuentes had died at a stranger's hand. Strangulation was too intimate. She exhaled and moved toward the dining room.

"Where are you going?" he asked.

She paused in the doorway. "To find a quote for the wedding."

He grinned. "Good luck."

Sparky shadowed her from the kitchen, through the dining and recreation rooms, and up the stairs to her office. With any luck, Google would deliver her an acceptable quote in no time and she'd be done worrying about that.

Chapter 20

Who knew searching for quotes about love and marriage would be so difficult. Colleen had spent nearly thirty minutes on the computer with no luck. She pushed her chair away from the desk and rolled it to the window. From her vantage point she caught glimpses of the dunes and the beautiful Atlantic Ocean in the distance. Sunlight flickered like jewels on the waves and a lightbulb went off in her head. Of course. Why had she not thought of it before? The shop window next to the jewelry store had that beautiful photograph of the ocean with a quote about love. It would be perfect. She verified on the computer that she had remembered the quote correctly, printed it, and slid the paper into her back pocket. She smiled, delighted with the quote and herself. She wouldn't be empty-handed at the wedding after all.

She descended the stairs to let Jimmy know she had succeeded in her love quote quest, checked his office, went out back to the area where they did drills, and found Chip planking on the asphalt with Bobby.

She had never heard of the planking exercise until Chip, ever the fitness fanatic, had introduced it to the house. The exercise consisted of lowering oneself onto one's forearms from a push-up position and holding that position for extended lengths of time. It wasn't until she had tried it herself that she appreciated the core strength it required to hold the body upright. She could see why Chip had picked it as an exercise for Bobby. Bobby's core could use a little firming.

Chip counted down, "Four, three, two, one."

As soon as "one" escaped Chip's lips, Bobby collapsed to the ground in a heap.

"Way to go, Big B," Chip said. He popped from the ground and helped Bobby up.

"You're trying to kill me, right?" Bobby said, but Colleen could tell that he was proud of his accomplishment.

"Hey, Chief. Did you see our guy?" Chip beamed, patting Bobby on the back.

"I did indeed," she said, amused by the pride Chip was taking in his pupil's progress.

The back door swung open and Aaron walked out. "Hey, man." Chip shook hands with the new arrival.

"Sorry I'm late," Aaron said. "I got held up at the stand with all the customers."

"No worries," Chip said.

"Hello, again," she said, surprised to see him. "What are you doing here?"

"Didn't I tell you? Aaron's catering the rehearsal dinner," Chip said with pride.

"That's wonderful," she said. "I'm glad you're here. I wanted to thank you for helping with our game day. Your food was a big hit."

"You give me too much credit," Aaron said, modestly.

"Isn't his barbecue the best?" Chip asked Bobby.

"I have the middle to prove it," Bobby joked and rubbed his belly.

"I guess it's not bad," Aaron said, knowing full well his food was tasty. "So you ready to chat about tomorrow tonight?"

"Actually," Colleen said, deciding to seize the opportunity to talk to the young man about his fellow worker Fuentes. "Before you guys get into the barbecue discussion, you mind if I ask you a few questions?"

"Okay," Aaron said, and gave Chip a puzzled look.

"Don't ask me," Chip said. "Bobby, you wanna try some pull-ups while the chief yaks with Aaron?"

"You are trying to kill me," Bobby said. He mouthed "Help me" to her and then moved several yards away to the bars with Chip.

The firehouse back door swung open again and Jimmy exited. "Oh, hey, Aaron," he said, joining them.

"Is this about my barbecue stand?" Aaron asked, concerned.

She shook her head. "I was hoping you could tell me about Michael Fuentes."

"What about him?"

"You both worked for Denny. Did you know him well?"

"We were friends for a while. Michael was a decent guy. Always had your back and was willing to help out if you needed an extra hand on the job."

"But then?" she asked, sensing from his tone there was more.

"Everything was cool and then he started distancing himself from us. When I asked him what was up he told me, nothing, but I could tell something was weighing on his mind."

"Did it have anything to do with work?" she asked. "Maybe with your boss Mr. Custis?"

"I got the feeling it was more personal. His mom was pretty sick. He had been trying to bring her to the States to get better treatment, but there were some immigration issues. That's why I didn't think much when he didn't come back to work after Christmas. I figured he'd gone down there to be with her and maybe things weren't going so well. Turns out . . ."

"It wasn't your fault what happened to Michael," Jimmy said.

"I knew something was wrong. I should have trusted my instincts, you know?" Aaron said, the distress evident in his voice.

She felt for the young man. It was obvious he had cared about his friend. "When you last saw Michael, was he having problems with anyone?" she asked, gently. "Anyone that might have had it in for him?"

Aaron shook his head. "What happened to him . . ." The muscles in his jaw tightened. "I'm sorry," he said after taking a breath. "It's just that after everything Michael had been through serving our country . . . Whoever did that deserves . . ."

Aaron exhaled. Jimmy patted his friend on the arm in sympathy.

She thought about the Snelling father and son. They were apparently capable of violence. Was it possible that the son had killed Denny and Fuentes? "Did Michael ever say anything to you about Greg Snelling or his father?"

"The tour company guys?" Aaron shook his head. "We all knew Denny and Snelling were in some kinda battle. Denny got super paranoid at one point. Started saying crazy things."

She wasn't surprised that a run-in with Snelling would make Denny angry. Putting those two men together would be like mixing volatile explosives in the same container.

"What kinda crazy things?" Jimmy asked.

"I don't remember it all; it was so bizarre. But there was this one day when Denny lined us all up, started yelling about smelling a rat, and then he sniffed us. Weird, right?"

Knowing what she did about Denny, she didn't imagine he would have taken too kindly to disloyalty. Now she wondered if it might have been Denny, not one of the Snellings, who had murdered Fuentes. She looked at Jimmy as if to ask "What do think?" He shook his head.

"What is it?" Aaron asked, noticing the exchange.

"Greg Snelling confessed to burning Salvatore's house and killing Custis," Jimmy said.

"Really?" he asked, wide-eyed. "You think Snelling . . ."

She shrugged. "That's why I asked if Michael knew them."

"Look," Aaron said. "I know sometimes good people can do bad things, make mistakes, but I can't imagine Michael doing anything to deserve what happened to him."

Chip dropped from the pull-up bars and approached, leaving a panting Bobby leaning against the poles behind him. "You done with my chef?" he asked, putting his arm around Aaron.

"He's all yours," she said. "Thank you, Aaron. I'm sorry about your friend."

Chip disappeared inside with Aaron. Bobby dragged himself by, waved, and entered the firehouse behind them.

"So?" Jimmy asked once they were gone.

"Things are more complicated than I thought," she said. "Aaron never said anything to you about what was going on?"

"Nope. Aaron's always been a loyal friend. I think the thought of not being there for Michael when he needed help has been tough on him."

She nodded. "I'm going to call Bill, see if he found out anything more about Fuentes," she said, pulling out her phone and heading around the side of the building.

"Where are you going?" Jimmy asked.

"To the beach. I need to clear my head." She whistled for Sparky. "Oh, by the way," she said. "I found my quote."

"Congratulations," he said with a grin.

She marched toward the boardwalk at Dolphin Street. Truthfully, she wanted to talk to Bill away from the firehouse. It wasn't that she didn't trust her men, but she didn't need them worrying about what was going on with the Fuentes case when they should be focused on events at the firehouse . . . and seeing the ocean really did help her think.

"What's up?" Bill asked, picking up on the second ring.

"I ran into Aaron," she said. "You know, the guy who runs the barbecue stand who used to work for Denny?"

"What did he have to say?"

"Fuentes may have been dealing with personal problems. You get a chance to talk to Denny's guys?"

"Yep."

"I'm going to the beach to walk Sparky. You wanna compare notes?"

"I'll be there in five minutes."

"I'll be near the stairs at Dolphin Street," she said and hung up. "Come on, boy," she called to Sparky, and jogged toward the beach.

Sparky loped after her, tongue out and tail swinging in a circle. They crossed Lighthouse Drive, sprinted over the boardwalk, and down the stairs.

"Taking Sparky for a run?" one of the lifeguards called down from his chair.

"Just a short one," she called back, and ran toward the surf and the hard wet sand. It would be good to shake out some of the tension in her neck.

Sparky dashed into the surf and then scampered out as the ocean washed up over his haunches. He ran in again and she stopped to let him have his fun playing in the waves. He was long overdue for a bath, maybe the seawater would help.

The waves washed toward her, stopping short of her feet, and she thought about Fuentes and how long he had been buried in the dune. If not for Tropical Storm Ana, he might still be there. He had clearly stumbled upon or become mixed up in something he shouldn't have, something that—to the killer—had high stakes. The Snellings and Custis seemed capable of killing but, as far as Aaron knew, his friend had had nothing to do with the tour company owner or his son . . . which left Denny as the most likely culprit. Could Fuentes have been the rat Denny was certain was in his midst?

She shook her head, baffled, and dodged Sparky's attempt to spray her with a shake of his fur. Maybe Bill would have some answers. She glanced at the stairs, saw him searching for her, and waved. He waved back and hiked toward her.

"Hey," he said, reaching her.

"Hey," she said, squinting up at him. It felt like forever since she had seen him. "Good to see you."

"You, too," he said with a smile. "Sparky's enjoying himself."

"If he comes too close, run. He's planning to get you as wet as he is."

"You wanna walk?" he asked, motioning up the beach.

She whistled for Sparky to join them. "So how'd it go with Denny's men?"

"A lot of complaints, mostly about superficial work things."

"And?"

"Denny's guys knew more about his business than I would have thought employees would know."

"How do you mean?"

"They knew about Denny's attempts to grab Pinky's land and that Snelling was after Denny's company."

"How is Snelling? Has he said anything more about why he killed Denny?"

"Not a word. He's still refusing to talk to his father and the lawyer. He'll be transferred to the detention center tomorrow."

"Aaron told me Denny accused his crew of having a rat in their midst. Given that everyone seemed to know Snelling was trying to make a grab for Denny's company, you think Denny suspected someone was spying on him and the business for Snelling?"

"It would make sense," he said.

"What did the other guys say about Fuentes?"

"Everyone liked him and seemed kinda shook up by the whole thing."

"Aaron had the same reaction," she said.

"Some heard Fuentes and Denny had had a run in."

"According to Aaron, Fuentes was upset about his mother being sick in Mexico. Maybe he wanted time off and Denny wouldn't give it to him. Did the guys say what the fight was about?"

He shook his head. They walked in silence and dodged incoming waves.

"So," Bill said. "About the wedding . . ."

"What about it?" she asked, yanked from her thoughts at his mention of a wedding.

"It's the day after tomorrow. You ready for your duties?"

She peered up at him and caught him grinning. "What's so amusing?"

"Nothing," he said, putting on an innocent face.

"For your information, I'm all good to go. I even have my quote ready." She yanked the paper with the quote from her back pocket and dangled it in front of him.

He attempted to grab the paper and she yanked it away. "You're not going to let me hear what you found?" he asked, surprised.

"You'll have to wait like everyone else."

"Okay," he said. He smiled at her affectionately and took her hand. "By the way, what time do you want me to pick you up?"

"What? Oh, I don't know," she said, distracted by the fact that they were now holding hands. They continued up the beach in silence, Sparky trotting beside them. They were the picture postcard of a happy couple walking down the beach . . . well, if that couple was a sheriff and a fire chief.

Chapter 21

"*Agent Morgan's* waiting to see you," Jimmy said as she walked into the engine bay after her beach stroll with Bill.

She hurried toward the door. "Why didn't you call?"

"I saw Bill's pickup at the boardwalk. I figured you were busy."

"Not that busy," she said. "How long has he been here?"

"Not long. Relax. He's been talking shop with the guys."

"Right." She entered the station. "Agent Morgan," she said, moving to greet the arson investigator, who sat wedged between Chip and Kenny in the middle of the sofa.

"Ah. There you are," Morgan said, extricating himself. "Thank you for the invitation, Chip. Most generous of you."

Colleen motioned for Morgan to join her in the engine bay. "I wish you had called. I hope you weren't waiting long."

"No. And for my time I've been rewarded with a wedding invitation."

"I'm so sorry," she said, mortified that Chip would invite the busy investigator to his wedding. "I'm afraid Chip is rather excited."

"As he should be."

"Please don't feel like you have to come."

"Why wouldn't I?" he asked. "Mrs. Morgan will be thrilled."

She raised her brows in surprise. Was the eccentric investigator seriously considering attending Chip's wedding? Out of curiosity, she half wished he would. She'd love to meet the woman who was his other half.

"So," he said. "You have evidence for me."

She led him to her SUV. "I tried to collect it as best I could but there wasn't much time."

She popped open the back and uncovered the paint, brush, bottle, and Ziploc-enclosed cigarette. Morgan lifted the Ziploc bag and peered at the cigarette.

"Greg Snelling was smoking that before he was apprehended."

"Matches or a lighter?" he asked. She gave him a puzzled look. "Did you see him light it?"

"No."

He nodded, removed a pen from his pocket, and with it drew the paint can and bottle toward the edge of the vehicle. He waved his hand over the containers, sniffed the wafting air, and then straightened up.

"This isn't your guy," he said, and returned the pen to his pocket.

"Don't you want to test it at the lab?"

"We'll do that, of course, but this isn't the accelerant."

"Are you sure?"

"This proboscis has never been wrong."

She didn't want to question Morgan—he was one of the most well-respected arson investigators in North Carolina—but if he didn't think the substances were consistent with their arson then they were back to square one.

He must have noticed her look of consternation. "If you don't believe my nose, what about your dog's? Sparky, isn't it? You said he reacted to the house and car fire scenes. Did he have the same reaction to these substances?"

"I didn't test it," she said.

"Then let's do that. Put it to the Sparky test. If his nose and my nose disagree I will reconsider."

"Okay," she said, figuring it was worth a shot.

"Wonderful. A little canine field test," he said, almost giddy. He grabbed the items she had collected from the Tour-zilla parking lot and set them up in a row on the ground several feet apart from one another. "Summon our scientist."

She suppressed a grin, spotted Sparky lounging in a hole he had dug by a bush, and whistled. He leapt from his hole and trotted toward them. When the dog was a few yards away, she held up her hand signaling him to stop. He cocked his head expectantly. There wasn't anything better to a Border collie than being given a task. Morgan nodded.

"Sparky, come," she said, and pointed to the objects on the ground.

Sparky dashed to the largest of the objects—the paint can—

cautiously sniffed, then moved on to the next item. After inspecting the last item he moved to Agent Morgan, sniffed him, and wagged his tail. Nothing had evoked the response from the dog that he had had at the fires.

"I believe Sparky and I are in agreement," Morgan said, and patted the dog on his rump. "Nevertheless, I will have these tested."

"So the guy we have locked up isn't our guy?" she asked.

"I'm not saying the guy you've got in custody didn't do it. I'm saying this isn't what he did it with."

"But why would someone confess to a crime he didn't commit?" she asked, now starting to doubt if Greg Snelling was their arsonist after all.

"You'll have to ask him," he said. "That's a different kinda species altogether."

He lifted some of the items from the ground and walked toward his car. She grabbed the rest and watched as he placed them into proper evidence collection containers.

"Tell me," she said. "What would you say our guy is like? If you had to take a guess?"

"White male, early to late twenties, works outdoors . . ."

"That sounds like Snelling," she said. But then again, it could be a lot of people. "Would you say he has issues with authority, like maybe his father?"

"Could be. I can tell you one thing . . . whoever set those fires certainly had problems with your victim." Morgan slammed his trunk closed. "Well, I best be on my way."

"Thank you for coming," she said. "I know we're a little out of the way."

"Well worth it," he said with a smile. "See you at the wedding."

"Right," she said, stepping aside with Sparky and waving as the agent drove off.

She had no idea why the man would attend a wedding of a complete stranger with his wife, but one thing she did know . . . she and Bill needed to question Greg Snelling again. She removed her phone from her pocket and dialed.

"Hey," she said after Bill picked up. "You at your office?"

"What's up?" he asked, sensing she had news.

"Morgan stopped by. He doesn't think what I collected from the Tour-zilla location is what was used in the arson."

"What are you saying?"

"I think we need to talk to Greg Snelling again, and I think we should have his father there."

"He's already refused to speak to his father," Bill said. "I don't see what—"

"Bill," she said, interrupting. "I'm not sure we have the right guy."

There was a pause on the other end and then . . . "How soon can you be here?"

"I'm on my way."

Chapter 22

"This better be worth my trip," Snelling said to Bill and Colleen in the hallway of the Sheriff's Department. "I've got a business to run."

Colleen was amazed. Never had she met a father who cared so little for a son.

"Thank you for coming," Bill said. "When do you think your lawyer will be here?"

"He's not coming," the Tour-zilla owner said.

"I'd advise you to—"

"I'm not paying no lawyer two-fifty an hour to be turned away again," Snelling said, cutting him off. "So what is this about?"

"I spoke with the agent in charge of the arson investigation," she said.

"We were hoping Greg could clear up some things for us before his transfer to detention," Bill said.

"So why talk to me?"

"We can't be certain," she said, "but we believe there's the possibility that your son didn't set the fire."

"What?"

"We're not saying he's innocent," Bill said. "But if he is, do you have any idea why he'd confess to something he didn't do?"

"Yeah," the man said. "Because he's a fool, that's why."

"Please, Mr. Snelling," she said, losing patience. "Your son could be innocent. If so, we'd like to know why he'd confess to a crime he didn't commit so we can catch the guy who did."

"And we think that can happen if you to speak to him," Bill said.

"We've been through this. He doesn't want to talk to me."

I wonder why, she thought. "Calling him an 'idiot' and 'fool' may not be helping."

Snelling raised a brow. "Have you met my son?"

"Do you really want him to go to jail?" she asked, stunned by the man's lack of feeling. "This is arson and murder."

"The chief's right," Bill said. "These aren't misdemeanors where he'll be out in twelve months."

Snelling considered what they had said. "All right. I'll talk to him. Don't know what good it will do, though."

"You sure you don't want to call your lawyer?" Bill asked.

"Yeah yeah. Let's get this over with."

"Right this way," Bill said, and led Snelling down the hall toward the interview rooms.

Bill and she had decided that an interrogation room might allow father and son to communicate freely without law enforcement personnel in the room to inhibit them. By having them meet in there rather than the holding area, they could observe the men from the other side of the two-way mirror and hear everything they said. With any luck, they'd find out Greg's motivations for either killing Denny or fabricating the story.

Bill reached the door. "We'll be observing, so don't try anything stupid or you'll be joining your son in the cell."

Snelling nodded.

Bill opened the door wide. "You got a visitor."

"Send him away," Greg said, seeing his dad.

"Just talk to your father, Greg," Bill said. The man didn't respond. "Do you want a lawyer present?"

Greg shook his head.

Bill motioned for Mr. Snelling to enter. As soon as he did so, she and Bill moved to the room next door where they could watch and listen.

"Hey," the father said, taking a seat in a chair opposite his son.

Greg turned his chair so that he faced away from his father and folded his arms.

"I'm talking to you," the father said, raising his voice.

"What's wrong with that man?" she muttered.

Bill looked at her with raised brows. "You're feeling bad for Greg?"

"Actually . . . yes."

"The cops think you may be lying . . . that you didn't rub out Custis like you said. Is that true?" asked the senior Snelling.

Greg stole a quick glimpse at his father. "What do you think?"

"I think only a chump—" Snelling stopped, glanced at the two-way mirror, and began again. "I don't understand why you'd do that."

Not great, Colleen thought about the father's tone with his son, but better. Bill turned the volume up on the speaker to the room.

Greg shifted in his chair to face his father. "Are you playing me, Dad?"

"Playing you?" Snelling said, puzzled. "What are you talking about?"

"Here we go," Bill said, quietly.

She held her breath. Their strategy had worked. The Snellings were communicating with one another. She crossed her fingers, hoping the father could maintain a civil tone with his son long enough that they could learn the truth.

"Don't you know?" the son asked, this time leaning closer to his father.

"Know what?"

The two men locked eyes, each seeking the truth, and then Greg's welled with tears and he looked away. The father slid his chair closer and took his son's jaw in his hand. Colleen tensed.

"Did you kill Custis?" the father asked. "I want the truth."

Greg paused a moment and then said, "No."

Snelling released his son's jaw. "Why'd you tell them you did?"

"Because," Greg said, wiping away a tear. "I thought you had."

"Why the hell would I do a dumb thing like that?" the father asked.

"You said Custis was on to us. That he knew you had someone snooping into his company. I thought—"

"What? That I'd kill the man to get it? Bring all that attention down on our business? Do I look like an ignoramus to you?"

Yes, Colleen silently answered. You've got a son that loves you enough to take the fall for murder and arson, throw way his future, and you can't see it.

Greg hung his head. "I didn't want you going to the pen."

She sighed. The only thing Greg was guilty of was trying to protect his unworthy father from going to jail.

"Wonder why he'd think that?" Bill asked.

"You think the father may have killed Custis?" she asked, surprised.

"His son obviously thought so. Gonna keep an eye on him."

Snelling peered at the two-way mirror. "I'll be calling our lawyer now."

Bill moved toward the door. "Fathers and sons," he said with empathy, and exited.

The door to the interview room opened. Bill signaled the father, took Greg by the arm, and escorted them out. She stared blankly at the empty interrogation room, mulling over the information of the last few hours.

Agent Morgan's and Sparky's noses had been correct. Snelling wasn't their suspect . . . which meant the arsonist and murderer was still out there. They were back to square one. Or were they? Snelling and Denny had been at odds over . . . What exactly had they been fighting about? Denny had been blackmailing Snelling over his tour company's interference with the horses as a way of getting Snelling to pay for use of the land. Snelling had apparently been prying into Denny's company—maybe even had someone on Denny's crew doing the snooping—provoking Denny's paranoia and suspicion that he had an informer amongst his employees.

Everything and everyone seemed to be connected to Denny and

his construction business. Even Denny's own men had had trouble with him. What about Fuentes? He had been an employee of Denny's. How had he felt about his boss? If the reactions of the other men were any indication, it wasn't positive. Fuentes had been long dead by the time Denny met his fate. Could the same person have killed both men? Or were they looking for more than one killer?

The door to the observation room opened. "You okay in here?" Rodney asked.

"Just thinking. Say," she said, suddenly remembering the comment Rodney had made about Denny on the beach. "You didn't care for Denny Custis. You mind telling me why?"

"Am I a suspect now?" he asked, good-humoredly.

"No," she said with a smile.

He leaned against the door, holding it open. "You ever encounter someone who rubs you the wrong way?"

"Sure. But if you don't mind my saying, it seemed like your feelings ran deeper than that."

"Let's just say I've known some Dennys in my life. They don't have a clue about things like loyalty, friendship, integrity, respect. In my opinion, that lack of understanding is what did Custis in."

"You could be right."

"So, are you done in here or should I bring you a chair to do more thinking?"

She chuckled. "I'm done." She exited and walked down the hall with the deputy.

"You ready for the wedding?" Rodney asked.

"Ready as I'll ever be," she said. "Fortunately, there's the rehearsal dinner, so I can practice."

"You'll be fine."

"Do you know me?" she said.

"Okay, maybe a little practice wouldn't hurt."

They laughed and Bill emerged from his office. "What's so funny?"

"Nothing," she said. Rodney gave her a quick wink and headed down the hall. "How are the Snellings?"

"The lawyer is on his way, but I'm still keeping my tabs on that father. If Greg is telling the truth then that means the older Snelling could be our strongest suspect."

Bill ran his hands through his hair. He was tired. Maybe it would be good to take a break.

"I've got to get back to the station, go over duty assignments, and pick up Sparky. You think you'll be done soon?"

"I wish. I told Rodney I'd stay on tonight." He lowered his voice. "But you know what I'm looking forward to?"

"What?"

"Spending time with you tomorrow night."

She blushed. "You're actually looking forward to the rehearsal dinner?"

"Sure. You'll be there and it will be a break from the case."

"I guess I'll see you at the rehearsal dinner then?"

The phone rang in his office. "You can count on it," he said, and crossed into his office to take the call.

She strolled from the building. She had a new errand to run at the TimBuck II shopping center before picking Sparky up from the firehouse and going home.

Chapter 23

As she drove through Carova on her way to the rehearsal dinner, Colleen recited the quote she had found for the wedding. She wasn't sure if she would be reading it tonight or only at tomorrow's ceremony. She should have paid more attention when Autumn had been explaining the schedule for Fawn and Chip's big day.

She traveled the road that led to Autumn's house and was surprised to find the dunes near Autumn's home lined with vehicles. She was twenty minutes early and yet it appeared everyone had beat her to the rehearsal dinner. Perhaps it was the excitement about the unique ceremony or the promise of Aaron's delicious North Carolina barbecue or the fact that people had carefully juggled schedules to be able to attend, but whatever the reason, it was evident by the early arrivals that everyone was eager to celebrate the special event.

She inched as far against the dune as she dared, leaving room for vehicles to drive by if necessary, and cut the engine. "Ready?" she asked Sparky, and he held up a paw. She checked the back bumper to be certain she wasn't blocking the road to the beach and strolled toward Autumn's house.

Sparky sniffed tires and grasses as they cleared the dune and reached Autumn's driveway. Colleen smiled. The celebrity statues lining the entrance had been adorned with flower crowns and necklaces and colorful balloons with ribbons had been tied to the wrists, giving the viewer the impression of musical notes floating to the heavens. Cool jazz and the smell of food cooking on a grill drifted from the ocean side. Sparky's nostrils twitched and he picked up his pace. She ducked under a string of decorative lights and followed Sparky, the music, and the sounds of merriment to the back.

"Hello!" Autumn called, an empty tray in hand. Sparky bounced toward the woman and inspected her sandals. "And who is this fella?"

"Sparky," she said. "I hope you don't mind that I brought him. I should have asked."

"Nonsense. All are welcome. Bring him tomorrow if you'd like."

Colleen felt a wave of guilt wash over her. How could she have suspected this woman?

"I see you're wearing the crystal," Autumn said.

"I thought I'd try it out. And don't worry, I won't be in these tomorrow," she said, indicating her jeans and boots.

"What's wrong with what you have on?" Autumn asked.

"I've been made aware that I need to expand my wardrobe," she said with a chuckle.

"Contrary to popular belief, clothes do not make the person. It's what's on the inside that counts."

"Well said."

"So," Autumn said. "Everyone is set up on the ocean side. I was just coming back to get more wine and beer."

"Would you like some extra hands?"

"No. Go mix," the woman said, gesturing toward the beach. "Antonio's inside. He'll help me."

The back door opened and Pinky emerged with a silver ice bucket and wine bottles. "Did I hear my name?" he asked, smiling down at them. "Ah, two visions of loveliness," he added, descending the stairs.

"He's such a flirt," Autumn said, tickled.

"Part of his charm," Colleen said.

"What can I say," he said, joining them. "I enjoy the company of interesting women."

"You sure you don't need any help?" Colleen asked.

Autumn tilted her head toward Colleen. "Is this one always so stubborn about not having fun?" she asked Pinky.

"Never beyond reason," he said.

"Okay, I'm going." Colleen mounted the stairs to locate the rest of the party.

She stole a look back and saw Pinky whisper in Autumn's ear, briefly rest his hand on the small of her back, and then remove it before anyone other than Colleen noticed. She grinned. There was something about a wedding that put everyone in the mood for love. She reached the top of the stairs. Cheers and calls of "There she is!" filled the air. She surveyed the crowd and spotted Bill yakking with Jimmy.

Card tables decorated with colorful tablecloths had been set up in an area between Autumn's house and the frontal dune that butted up against the beach. A short distance away, Aaron and Bobby were cooking on a grill. Chip and Fawn's friends gathered around the couple sharing stories, and Pastor Fred from the Corolla Chapel was huddled in deep conversation with Chip's parents. Beyond the tables and dinner participants stood the gazebo, outfitted with ribbons that billowed in the ocean breeze. She descended and joined Bill and Jimmy.

"You made it," Bill said.

"We were starting to worry," Jimmy added.

"I'm early," she said, feeling defensive even though she knew Jimmy was teasing.

"Are you actually wearing a necklace?" Jimmy asked, and reached to inspect it.

"Would you stop," she said, blocking his hand.

"Seriously, it's nice." He moved away to talk to Chip and the other guys.

"You see the grief I get?" she asked Bill.

"You want me to say something?" he asked in a stern voice as if he would reprimand Jimmy.

She smiled, knowing he wasn't serious. The dinner was a welcome break from the investigations. She observed the guests. "I see Pastor Fred will be presiding. I'm surprised."

"Why's that?" he asked.

"It's rather traditional for those two," she said, indicating the happy couple.

Fawn and Chip laughed at something a friend had said. Fawn spied Colleen and excused herself from the group.

"I'm so pleased you're here," Fawn said to Colleen. "I see you're wearing the necklace Aunt Autumn made you."

"I didn't know she made it," Colleen said, and inspected the necklace with new appreciation.

"With a little input from me," Fawn said, proudly.

"Of course. My pink aura," she said, and winked at Bill.

"Exactly!" Fawn said, delighted. "You know, Sheriff, I can read your aura, too, if you'd like. To make sure you two are compatible."

Bill's cheeks flushed a deep red. "I think I'll leave a little to mystery."

"Ah, yes," Fawn said. "That's fun, too."

"Fawn," called Chip. "You never told me you wore braces."

"Are they telling stories on me?" she asked, and left to celebrate with her friends.

Autumn and Pinky appeared at the top of the stairs. "Is everyone ready for the rehearsal?" Autumn called down to them.

The group enthusiastically responded in the affirmative.

Pastor Fred excused himself from his conversation with Chip's parents and motioned for Fawn and Chip to accompany him. "If everyone is ready, I'd like to begin going over the ceremony, or rather spiritual union as the young lady has requested I call it."

Fawn beamed and Colleen suppressed a grin.

"Will the wedding party please join me," Pastor Fred continued.

"I guess that's me," she whispered to Bill, and joined Autumn, two of Fawn's friends, and the guys from the station who were Chip's groomsmen.

"Guests, please follow the wedding party."

Colleen peeped over her shoulder at Bill and found him in conversation with Pinky.

"What do you think they're talking about?" Autumn said, noticing her watching Bill and Pinky.

"Sports," Colleen said.

Autumn giggled. "You could be right."

Pastor Fred led the group to the gazebo and then, to Colleen's surprise, down the stairs to the beach. She had expected Fawn and Chip to take their vows in the decorated structure but soon learned that the couple wanted everyone gathered around them in a "circle of love" and the only place there was room to do that was on the beach.

For the next half hour, Pastor Fred steered them through the order of events, where to stand, who the groomsmen should escort and when, and the vows. True to his reputation, he had also found a Hallmark greeting card quote, but in the spirit of keeping the love quotes a surprise until the wedding, decided to wait until the special day itself to share it along with all the others. There was a final, stern request from Fred for everyone to arrive early tomorrow . . . and by early he meant before the sun came up. If all went well and Mother Nature cooperated, the plan was for Fawn and Chip to be officially declared united in marriage as the sun broke over the Atlantic Ocean—a new day for their new beginning together.

As Fred finished the last of his instructions, the group was treated to the unexpected arrival of wild horses. They emerged from behind a nearby dune, noted the wedding party's presence, and then ambled toward the ocean.

"Too bad we can't have that happen tomorrow morning," someone said, voicing the silent wish of many.

"If it's God's will," Fred said with a smile. "Any questions before we eat?" Silence. "Very good then. Let's dine."

The party eagerly returned to the tables where Aaron had already set them with covered dishes of steaming barbecue chicken, pulled pork, as well as salad, steamed vegetables, and fruit for the vegetarians. Soon corks were popped and everyone dug into the food.

Colleen heard Sparky whimpering and scanned the tables. The last thing she wanted was her canine friend begging guests for food. She spotted the dog sitting attentively by Aaron's side at the grill, tail wagging. Aaron took a piece of chicken from his plate, placed it in his palm, and fed it to Sparky. The dog devoured the treat in seconds and raised his paw for more. Aaron shook the dog's paw and reached for another piece of food. Time to rescue the chef from her pesky friend.

"Excuse me," she said to Bill, and left the table to retrieve her little beggar. "Sorry about that," she said, approaching Aaron. She took Sparky by the collar and attached his leash. "He really does know better."

"It's actually my fault. He kept me company while I cooked so I thought I'd give him a little reward. I hope you don't mind."

Sparky tugged on the restraint and pawed furiously at the foot of the grill. "No." She pulled Sparky away from the grill. "But I think you may have created a bit of a monster," she said, and chuckled.

"My most enthusiastic review so far," Aaron said, truly pleased.

"You did a wonderful job," she said. "Okay, Sparky, let's give Aaron a break."

She returned to her seat and tied Sparky to her chair to keep him out of the chef's way. Her canine buddy positioned himself at her feet and focused on the grill. It would be hard to get him to go back to his usual dog food.

She and Bill shared a table with Autumn, Pinky, and Jimmy. She had been skeptical about the mix, but it resulted in a surprisingly pleasant combination with a variety of opinions that made for lively conversation and debate. Perhaps because the occasion was festive, everyone was friendly about their differences, and it was fun listening to people who saw the world in a completely different way from her. Who, after all, wants to sit at a table with people who think exactly like you?

There were numerous compliments to the chef throughout the meal. Aaron radiated with pride and moved away from the hot grill to have a much deserved smoke. He pulled out matches, lit the cigarette, dropped the match in the sand, rubbed it out and—in a sudden flash—all the pieces of the puzzle came together. The cigarette smoke Myrtle had smelled. The matches found at the house. Agent Morgan's discussion of accelerants used in cooking. Sparky's reaction at the fire sites and tonight at the grill. Aaron's employment with Denny's company and his agitation while discussing Fuentes' death with Jimmy and her at the station. What was it that Aaron had said about the person who had murdered his friend? "Whoever did that deserves . . ." Now she understood that what Aaron had meant was that Michael's murderer deserved punishment.

She leaned toward Bill and whispered in his ear. Bill subtly peeked at Aaron, nodded, and rose.

"Hey, Aaron, great meal," Bill said, approaching the man.

"Thanks," Aaron said, beaming.

"You mind if I ask you a couple questions?'"

Aaron looked around at the party—puzzled, saw everyone having a good time, relaxed, and then noticed Colleen studying him. "Sure. Let me wash my hands and I'll be right back," he said and walked toward the house.

"If you'll excuse me," she said to her table. "I'm going to take Sparky for a quick walk for doggie business."

Pinky, Autumn, and Jimmy waved halfheartedly, distracted by their conversation. None of the partygoers noticed Bill and Colleen shadow Aaron up the stairs . . . none except Aaron.

"He's gonna make a run for it," Bill said, and picked up his pace.

As soon as Aaron was out of sight of the party, he took off, jumped into his Jeep, and peeled away down Autumn's driveway. Bill, Colleen, and Sparky dashed toward the vehicles parked along the road.

Bill skidded to a halt. His pickup had been blocked in. "Damn," he said under his breath.

"We'll take mine," Colleen called, and they sprinted to her SUV.

She flung open her door and Sparky leapt in. Bill was already in the passenger seat as she slid in and started the engine.

"He's heading down the beach," Bill said, watching the Jeep disappear toward the ocean.

She shifted into reverse, thankful she had parked at the intersection of two roads so that nobody could park behind her, and hit the gas. Sand flew from under the tires and they jolted back. She switched gears and zoomed toward the beach.

They rolled out of the community. "There he is," Bill said, pointing through the windshield.

"I see him," she said, and flipped on her emergency lights and siren.

She zipped onto the wet sand and hit the gas, pushing the SUV above the speed limit of fifteen miles per hour—something she'd never normally do but, given the circumstances, felt was warranted. Still, she was careful to keep an eye out for dogs, children, horses, fishermen, and people walking on the beach.

She swiftly closed the gap between them and the Jeep. Please, don't let anyone get hurt, she thought, and then, as if her worst fear was coming true, a stallion with a harem and foal emerged from over the dunes and headed straight for the water in the path of the Jeep.

Aaron must have seen the horses, too, because the Jeep swerved left, slammed into one of the ancient stumps protruding from the sand, flipped on its side, and slid to a halt. She slowed and hit the brakes. Bill bolted, Colleen fast on his heels. Sparky took off after the horses. She reached the overturned Jeep seconds after Bill.

"I didn't mean to do it," Aaron said as he bled from an ugly gash in his forehead. "It was an accident."

The ocean washed into the Jeep, flooded the interior and then retreated, dragging the Jeep with it.

"We should get him out of there," she said.

They grabbed Aaron under the arms and lugged him out and away from the Jeep. Another wave crashed ashore and this time the Jeep became partially submerged. Sparky barked repeatedly and nipped at the horses legs, herding them back into the dunes to safety.

"Aaron Lacy, you're under the arrest for the murder of Denny Custis and Michael Fuentes," Bill said.

"No!" Aaron attempted to stand but collapsed in the sand.

She kneeled to examine the wound and check his awareness. "Follow my finger," she said, and he did as instructed.

"You gotta believe me," he said to her, and then looked up at Bill. "Denny killed Michael. When I confronted Denny, he attacked me. I've got it all recorded on my phone. Along with his confession. I swear."

"What about the fire?" Bill asked, unconvinced.

"Denny was going to burn Salvatore's place. I went along so I could get him alone, trick him into confessing what he did to Michael. After . . . well, I panicked. I never meant for any of this to happen."

Tears welled in his eyes and then, to her surprise, the man began to sob. What a shame, she thought. If Aaron had gone to Bill with his suspicions about Denny killing his friend instead of taking matters into his own hands, all of this could have been prevented. She could tell from Bill's expression that he was thinking the same.

Bill helped Aaron to his feet. "Aaron Lacy, you're under arrest for arson and the murder of Denny Custis."

Aaron's shoulders relaxed and Colleen sensed relief wash over him now that the truth was known. It wasn't how she would have liked things to turn out, but finally the arson and murder cases had been solved.

Chapter 24

"You think you can stay clean until after the wedding?" Colleen asked Sparky as she brushed his fur in the living room.

After the rehearsal dinner and Aaron's arrest, she had left Bill at the station to take Aaron's statement. It had been a long night. True to his word, Aaron had recorded a complete confession on his phone from Denny about killing Michael Fuentes. Denny and Fuentes had indeed had a run-in after Fuentes had asked Denny for time off and money to take care of his ailing mother in Mexico. When Denny had refused, Fuentes had agreed to steal and make copies of confidential documents about Denny's business for Snelling. Why his friend didn't come to him to borrow the money, Aaron would never know. Snelling paid Fuentes for spying on Denny, which gave Michael the money he needed for his mother's medical care. Unfortunately, Denny figured out Fuentes had been the rat and it had cost Fuentes his life. It wasn't until his friend's body had been discovered under the walkway and the death ruled a homicide that Aaron had suspected that Denny had killed him.

On the morning of Pinky's house fire, Denny had picked Aaron up at his barbecue stand and asked him to bring charcoal lighter fluid—the alcohol-based accelerant—with him. When Aaron arrived at the house with Denny, he realized that Denny was there to burn Pinky's property down and pretended to go along, figuring he'd win Denny's trust because he was about to help his boss commit arson. Then Myrtle showed up unexpectedly, smelled the cigarette he had been smoking, argued about the horses, and left. Because his phone had still been on, parts of that conversation, too, were recorded, and confirmed what Myrtle and Jacob had reported earlier. After Myrtle's departure, Aaron had told Denny he was going to the police with the confession and Denny attacked him. In their struggle, Denny fell, hit his head, and stopped breathing. Panicked, Aaron grabbed the charcoal lighter fluid, doused the house, lit it, took off in Denny's pickup, ditched the truck, and walked home. Later, when he realized Colleen and Bill were getting close to figuring out what had happened, he returned to the pickup and burned that as well. At the end of hearing it all, Colleen had sighed. It had been a series of bad decisions that had led to a young man perhaps spending the rest of his life in jail . . . all because he wanted justice for a friend. She hoped, somehow, a judge or jury would take pity on him.

When she had arrived home last night she had been so keyed up by the events of the evening that she had been unable to sleep. That's when she had decided to give Sparky his much-needed bath.

He was, after all, an invited wedding guest, and she couldn't have him showing up smelly for Fawn and Chip's big day.

She gave the dog's coat a final brush. Sparky wagged his tail and tried to lick her face. Smokey apparently found the clean dog smell appealing, and groomed a section of his fur, wanting to do her share in getting her friend ready. Colleen crossed to the secretary desk in her living room, retrieved a wide royal blue ribbon, cut the ends at an angle, and tied the ribbon around his neck.

"The finishing touch," she said, and stepped back to do a final inspection. "You really are a handsome dog," she said, pleased.

She noted the time on the cable box. Five o'clock. It was still dark but the sun would come up fast and she needed to allow time to get to Carova. The last thing she wanted was to disappoint Fawn and Chip or to have Pastor Fred scold her. She did a final check in the mirror. The necklace Autumn had given her was a pretty accessory to her new outfit. Won't Bill be surprised, she thought, satisfied with her appearance, and then exited with Sparky. Seconds later she burst back into the house. Smokey looked at her as if to say "Back so soon?" She retrieved the paper with the love quote from the kitchen counter, rubbed the cat's back, and dashed out again. Time for a wedding!

She left Route 12 and drove onto the four-wheel-drive beach highway. Up ahead she saw a caravan of headlights slowly making their way up the beach and then noticed more falling in behind her. Something about the procession of the lights gave her goose bumps. Each set of lights represented someone wishing to celebrate Fawn and Chip's love for one another. She took back all the grumbling of this morning about having to get up so early. This ceremony was going to be something special.

She followed the lights up the beach. They shifted left and then suddenly extinguished as vehicles disappeared behind the dunes and into the community. She wondered where Bill was in the caravan and if he had been able to get home to get a couple hours of sleep. She and Bill had planned to go to the wedding together, but with Aaron's arrest last night and the uncertainty of Bill being able to get away, they had agreed it would be better to meet there. At first she had been let down that they weren't arriving together, but now she was glad. Her appearance would be a surprise—one she hoped he would like.

She parked behind the car that had been traveling down the beach in advance of her, exited, and heard the murmur of excited voices. She squinted, trying to make out who had already arrived.

"You're going too fast. Slow down," she heard a familiar voice say in front of her.

"I can't be late, Mother," came the response.

That could only be one mother and son duo—Myrtle and Bobby.

"Why don't you go ahead," came Nellie's voice. "Myrtle and I will be fine."

"Good morning," she said, catching up to the women.

"Oh, good morning," Nellie said. "Is that Sparky with you?"

Sparky panted loudly at the sound of his name.

"Bobby told us about the Lacy boy," Myrtle said. "Too bad. He was a good kid."

"Which makes it all the more unfortunate," Colleen said.

"Wonder what coulda got into him," Myrtle said as they walked toward the LED lights strung up in Autumn's driveway.

"We'll have plenty of time to speculate about that later," Nellie said. They moved along the lit driveway. "Isn't this lovely?"

Colleen didn't know how Autumn had managed it, but the balloons that had been tied around the statues' wrists were now lit from the inside and bobbed in the breeze like champagne bubbles.

"At least I can see now," Myrtle said. "Why couldn't they have done this at a normal hour?"

"Because then it wouldn't be a sunrise wedding," Colleen said.

"I think it's nice," Nellie said.

"Hmpf," Myrtle said, eyeballing the statues.

Nellie chuckled and took Myrtle's arm. "I see I'm bringing the crab to the beach."

"Nell!" Myrtle exclaimed, then snorted a laugh and squeezed her friend's arm.

"I'll leave you ladies to visit with the others," she said, impressed that Nellie had put Myrtle in a lighter frame of mind.

She went in search of Autumn, peered out back, and found the woman bustling about looking somewhat distraught. "Thank goodness you're here," Autumn said dashing toward her. "My don't you look nice," she added, nodding with approval.

"Thank you," Colleen said. "You don't look too bad yourself."

"Yeah? I should have worn bright orange to get everyone's attention. I haven't had any luck getting folks down to the beach. Maybe they'll listen to you. You mind?"

"Not at all."

She didn't know how her requests would have any more sway than Autumn's entreaties, but she put on her best chief voice and for the next half hour helped Autumn and Pinky corral the wedding party and guests down to the beach—as it turned out, no easy task as people were busy socializing about the wedding and occasionally whispering about "poor Aaron Lacy's" arrest. Even Sparky managed to round up a few guests to the spot where Pastor Fred would preside. The sky was lightening. If all was to go according to plan they'd need to begin soon.

"Has anyone seen the pastor?" Autumn asked, panic creeping into her voice.

"You keep everyone here," Colleen said. "I'll go see if he's wandering around up front."

Colleen jogged up the stairs, reached the top, and stopped. Heading up the stairs was Bill. The ocean wind blew at her back, causing her beige blouse and pale blue cotton skirt to billow around her. She froze. He climbed the stairs and she self-consciously tugged at her skirt.

Pinky rushed from the house with the bouquet Fawn had forgotten inside, saw Colleen gazing at Bill, said, "You're a lucky man" to Bill, dashed by her with a wink, and hurried to the beach.

"You look beautiful," Bill said.

She should have said thank you, but she wasn't accustomed to being told she was beautiful, so she stood there with a dumb smile on her face.

"Am I the last to arrive?" he asked, bringing her back to the moment.

"No. We're waiting for Pastor Fred."

"After the lecture he gave us about being late?" he asked, astonished, and they both laughed.

She peered over her shoulder back at the horizon. The sky was lightening. "If he doesn't get here soon, you might have to do the honors," she said, and smiled when his face paled. "I'm kidding. I'm sure he'll be here."

As if on cue, Pastor Fred appeared from behind the house and raced toward them. "I'm here!" he called. "I'm coming!"

"Would it be right to tease a pastor?" she asked Bill as the man climbed the stairs.

"No," he said, amused. "Guess we better get down to the beach."

She and Bill rapidly descended the steps. The group cheered when Fred appeared at the top of the stairs. Sparky joined in with several barks.

Pastor Fred scrambled to the shore, positioned himself with his back to the ocean at the top of the circle of people, and inhaled deeply. "Everyone, take your places," he said. A giggle rippled over the gathering. They had been in their places for some time.

"Music please," Fred said.

One of Fawn's friends strummed a ukulele and then, much to everyone's astonishment and delight, Myrtle and Pinky began to softly sing, "Somewhere . . . over the rainbow . . ." in perfect harmony. Colleen was amazed. Pinky was right . . . Myrtle did have a lovely voice.

Kenny, Bobby, and the guys escorted Fawn's girlfriends, Colleen, and Autumn to the ocean side of the circle. Colleen gazed over the group and spotted Rodney, the parents, and then Agent Morgan. The investigator waved, pointed to the good-looking woman next to him, and mouthed "Mrs. Morgan." She smiled, gave a slight nod, surveyed the rest of the joyful group, and discovered Bill beaming at her. She felt her cheeks flush the color of the crystal around her neck, but she didn't care. She was happy—and people were supposed to be happy at weddings.

"I believe you're next," she heard Fred say, and all eyes were on her.

"What?" she asked.

"Your quote for the bride and groom," Autumn whispered.

"Oh right." She reached into her skirt pocket, retrieved the paper, and cleared her throat. "This is a quote by Maharishi Mahesh Yogi that I think is not only good advice for Fawn and Chip, but perhaps for all of us." She took a breath and read, "'Let not the din of the world, and the thick and thin of life, disturb the fullness of love in us. Let us be full of grace, and full of light.'"

She folded the paper and glanced at the bride and groom. Fawn's eyes welled with tears and Chip gave her a thumbs-up. She caught Jimmy grinning at her with pride. See, she thought, I do have a heart.

"That was lovely," Fred said, removing a card from his jacket pocket. "And now I, too, would like to read."

Chip leaned toward the pastor and said, "I don't mean to tell you your job, Pastor, but I think you might have to get to it."

She glanced at the ocean. It was true. Any minute now the sun would peek its glorious crown over the horizon.

"It appears the good Lord wishes me to get on with it," Pastor Fred said.

A wave of good-natured giggles rippled over the party. Attention shifted to witness Fawn's and Chip's vows to one another. When Chip removed the ring from his pocket and presented it to Fawn, she gasped, kissed him, and then quickly apologized to Fred for "skipping ahead."

Finally, the moment came. Pastor Fred turned to the assemblage and pronounced Chip and Fawn husband and wife as the sun burst over the horizon. A brilliant orange glow flooded the sky, the gathering applauded, cell phones and cameras clicked, and Fawn and Chip embraced in a long, sweet kiss. Colleen searched for Bill, who was standing on the perimeter of the circle. He waved and smiled warmly at her, his eyes wrinkling at the edges in the way she loved. There was only one wedding she could imagine that could be more perfect.